The Freedom Factory

Ksenia Buksha

Translated by Anne O. Fisher

Original Illustrations by the Author

PHONEME
MEDIA

Praise for *The Freedom Factory*

"Frankly, it is not hard to understand why *The Freedom Factory*, written by Ksenia Buksha, won Russia's National Bestseller Award in 2014... [and readers] will have the privilege to appreciate the fluidity and profound humanity of this book."
—**Lou Sarabadzic**, *Asymptote*

"In poignant and lyrical prose, Ksenia Buksha's *The Freedom Factory* renders the history of a real military factory in St. Petersburg... sometimes humorous and at other times heartbreaking." —**Meagan Logsdon**, *Foreword Reviews*

"Ksenia Buksha's *The Freedom Factory* is not only a brave reconstruction of the Soviet 'construction novel' of the 1920s and '30s, it is a bravura attempt to capture the polyvocal soul of the Soviet experience. Buksha writes like Svetlana Alexievich possessed by the spirit of Samuel Beckett, and Annie Fisher's expertly modulated, impressively resourceful translation communicates the effect of her style in full."
—**Boris Dralyuk, co-editor,** *The Penguin Book of Russian Poetry*

"*The Freedom Factory* presents an unusual, deeply human kaleidoscope of lives in the Soviet Union. As if the factory itself witnesses the stories that unfold inside it, the reader encounters fragments of conversation that skip through time and rarely come to any resolution. The images of experience are variously positive and negative and sometimes tragic, often against the background of older characters' recollections

of the Siege of Leningrad. Anne O. Fisher's translation from the Russian is supple and effective, catching the tone of the conversations, personal or bound to the workday. In a society where labor was the basis of social policy, it is no surprise that so many aspects of life come up between these covers—inside or around the walls of the factory."
—Sibelan S. Forrester, Professor of Russian Language and Literature, Swarthmore College

"*The Freedom Factory* is a thriller, a romance, and a social drama all in one, and—this is especially important—it's a book by a post-Soviet person about the Soviet experience."
—Dmitry Bykov, winner of the Big Book prize

"My first impression was that of a ... novel written by a slightly drunk Joyce."
—Maxim Amelin, Solzhenitsyn Prize and Poet Prize winner

"[When I read the novel] I thought of Spanish Nobel laureate Camilo José Cela and his novel *The Hive*... which through the blending of many disparate voices gives an image of the time, the characters, the particular atmosphere. *The Freedom Factory* has echoes of this same device."
—Gennady Kalashnikov, poet

"Ksenia Buksha has successfully done what no one else, it seems has been able to do: combine utopia and dystopia."
—Nadezhda Sergeyeva, *Zvezda*

Phoneme Media
P.O. Box 411272
Los Angeles, CA 90041

Copyright © 2014 by Ksenia Buksha
Translation © 2017 by Anne O. Fisher

ISBN: 978-1-944700-15-7

This book is distributed by Publishers Group West

Cover Art by Ksenia Buksha
Cover design and typesetting by Jaya Nicely

Printed in the United States of America

Published with the support of the Institute for Literary Translation (Russia)

ИНСТИТУТ ПЕРЕВОДА

AD VERBUM

Phoneme Media is a nonprofit media company dedicated to
promoting cross-cultural understanding, connecting people and
ideas through translated books and films.

http://phonememedia.org

To Mark and Sasha,
without whom this book wouldn't exist either

Table of Contents

The Freedom Factory

1.

The Central Tower

Well, one smart mother did instill it in her first-grade son: when you see those letters, white on red, don't read them, it's pure nonsense—but don't you tell anybody what I just told you. Pure nonsense, in white letters on red, right there above the Freedom Factory. A spotlight over the entrance points its beam directly up. Multitudes of snowflakes, tiny as sparks, keep flying into the beam and swirling around like burning gunpowder. The factory workers hurry home in this freezing cold, holding their breath, to ring in the New Year. The snow doesn't just crackle under their feet, it actually squeals. In this kind of cold, breathing is impossible: you might as well try to breathe black pepper. It feels like the snow would catch fire if you held a match to it. And no looking up, either, not a chance, although if you do go ahead and try to lift your frost-burned face you'll see a red banner over the entrance, and white letters, and above them the spotlight's beam, drilling through the murky, sleepy sky over the Narva Outpost all the way into outer space, although its target really isn't outer space at all, but the clock on the Central Tower, that's what! The time on the clock is five to ten, but the snow-covered cornices and ledges crowning both the Central Tower itself and the entire recently restored main building gleam white.

Comrades! A clapping of hands gets everyone's attention, and he breaks into the old song: "Five minutes! Five mi-i-inu-u-utes!" No, don't worry, we've still got two hours. What I mean is that in five minutes we will get ready to go and wish each other a Happy New Year, and then we will exit the shop in an orderly fashion, hop on the tram, and be home in time to hear the clock strike twelve on the radio. Attention, attention!

D (a skinny red-head) contends that the module has to be assembled this year, not left until next year. His childhood friend, Q, contends that… Olya! Let's spend the New Year together. The whole year? Oh, sorry about that, I meant to say, New Year's Eve. Although now you mention it, I would spend the whole year with you, Olenka, if you were up for it. I'd rather spend it with D. He's just as much of an idiot as you, but at least he shuts up sometimes. Well sure, of course we'll take D with us! We'll all head over to my place. My dad's on duty, he'll be gone all night. I'll take care of the, you know, the stuff. Come on, D, quit your dawdling and finish it, or else the trams'll stop running. The trams run until eleven (setting a sprocket in graphite lubricant). I'll be right there. You go on and invite Olya over. I did, I already did! Is that so? When was that?

It's freezing outside, enough to knock the wind out of you. I can't remember it ever being this cold. I can't either. They say it was during the blockade, but I don't remember. Man, when we lived in the Urals, minus forty-five in the winter was no big deal. But at least the air was dry there. Here you've got this mist, this haze. My grandma's been wheezing for three days, she can't take this kind of freezing cold. Then she shouldn't go outside. No, she wheezes inside, too.

Whoa, the light's on in number four. Hey boys, let's go check out Four, what'd they do over there? I haven't seen it yet. But what's the time? We got plenty of time. Let's go.

Shop Four's new, expansive layout. Out past the enormous windows, just touched by frost, the sharp outlines of bare branches. Booming footsteps. An echo reverberates. Get a load of that! What kind of machines are those, anyway? They're, like, war trophies. Careful, boys. Someone's coming.

It's okay, chief, we're from Fifteen. Showing the girl around. It's all fancy-schmancy over here now, isn't it? (Felt boots, baggy overcoat, moustache.) Happy New Year! Olya's smile, now, for a smile like that you'd do anything! Olya's with the quality control department. Ah, I see. Happy New Year, kids. That's right. There's certainly something worth looking at here, that's right. And here I was, thinking, who are those folks? You make sure to come by again. 'Cause next time I'll... So you're from Fifteen, then, the hardest-working shop, always working late. Puts in the most overtime. (A whiff of alcohol.) Go on and take a seat. We'll have us a little chat. That tram won't get away from you. There's a lot I can tell you about... I was here way back when there wasn't anything here, nothing at all, but I was here... Wanna know what I did? I kept this factory from burning down. That's something you don't know. During the war, that's right. Come on, now, have a seat. You Komsomol kids! Listen up, I'm gonna tell you how it happened, 'cause you don't know a thing about it.

It was spring by the time we put out the Freedom fire, it was back in... that's right, it was back in May of forty-two, I think. This here was a textile factory back then. That's right... a fougasse set it on fire, and then at five in the evening the artillery started shelling us. They really let us have it, that's right... And here we are, under fire, putting out a fire, it was crazy. There were twenty fire crews on hand, the entire Narva Outpost came out, basically... we get here and everything's burning, from the first floor to the last. Children came running out at us, led by their teachers... there was a preschool there, you can just imagine… they'd brought in orphans from all over the outpost. I tell Dimka, you cover those buildings there. I knew the cotton warehouse was in there, it was just awful. The power plant was there too, and if that'd caught fire… Dimka and his men ran over there, but we took the main building… it was burning stronger and stronger as we watched. The workshops were full of cotton, burning cotton came busting out the windows, there was oily sludge inside, all the flooring in a factory's soaked in oil, and the fire swallowed it up like paper. We sent the young officers in training to put out the repair shop on the second floor, we thought it'd be safer, while we went up to the fourth floor… then a shell hits the side of the building, pow! and all those youngsters were laid out, just gone… but we didn't know it at the time, no way to tell what was going on. Beams are coming down, the pump's hit by a shell so there's no water, the hoses are torn… And then I look up and the roof's coming down. That's it, let's go, I say, and we make it down to the second story, but there's no stairs, can't see anything… There was this one fellow, Yegor Gelfin, he died later at the front… he just jumped down there, blind, can you imagine that? That's how he helped get us out. Now that's a feat! And I came out last! I got snagged on something, I have no idea what's going on, I'm all but deaf, but I keep pushing on, the flooring's already crackling right behind me, and as soon as I jump out the whole thing came crashing down! But we saved two stories, and Dimka saved the cotton warehouse; if that'd gone up we'd've been surrounded, it would've done us all in. When there's that much fuel, the air itself just catches fire and sucks everything in, like a funnel; that would've been the end, period! But no… we saved the cotton warehouse, and all the outbuildings, you can see yourself this is all old… we saved the factory… we lost eight fighters. That's right…

You're a hero, chief! Who, me? (cough) Come on, now, a hero... (cough) Let's say I'm a hero of the past. And you are the heroes of the future. Better think twice about picking a fight with us, am I right? Comrades, this is great and all, but the last tram is leaving in five minutes. Goodbye! Goodbye! Happy New Year!

It's hard to run in the freezing cold. Your face burns, and the tiniest little snowflakes sear your cheeks and blow in sparkling flurries up under the hem of your coat. They can already hear the muffled clatter in the dark as they come running off Volynkina onto Kalinin. A headlight comes around the corner. They race to the stop as fast as they can, Q dragging Olya by the hand, they spring into the tram, the doors close... and only then do they realize that D had long ago fallen behind. There goes his lanky, disheveled frame, muttonchops frosted over, fur hat askew. The tram picks up speed.

You left him behind, Q! What, is it my fault he runs so slow? I just thought he was right there with us. You should've grabbed his hand too! Listen, Olenka, if you think about it, what do we need that red-headed weirdo for, anyway? Aren't we better off without him? It's like they say: if you snooze, you lose. The tram comes to a halt: just a short distance between stops here, twelve buildings, one intersection... Olya jumps out into the empty, snowy road, into crackling sparks, the snow is bright orange under the streetlight like the ice in a skating rink, and out above the treetops in Ekaterinhof Park the black cube of the Central Tower rises up into the murky sky, topped by a bright column of light, and while the tram lurches off with a rattle, carrying Q into the gelid gloom along Bypass Canal, Olga walks briskly forward, as D's spare frame treads toward her; he's beginning to make her out, but now we can't see them anymore.

2.

Tasya

Ta-a-asya, Boris Izrailyevich croaks, and the unspoken but undeniable malediction, directed at no one in particular, hangs briefly in the air. So you're Tasya. Holding her personal file up close to his face, the personnel manager reads: born 1942, place of birth Leningrad, parents unknown. Boris Izrailyevich frowns. The Siege. He involuntarily pictures the frost-coated floorboards, the walls scraped almost bare of wallpaper, and the like. I'm from an orphanage. So you're fresh out of factory apprenticeship school, then? Yes. Did they send you? Assign you here? No, I wanted to come. I want to work at an electronics factory. Boris Izrailyevich looks up. Why, that's marvelous! Let's go, I'll show you around. Now what kind of job can we set you up with? We could take you on as an apprentice press operator in Shop Twelve. There's a lot of girls there, you'll make friends. Oh, yes, I'd like that!

They stride through the courtyard. One limps, the other minces. Gee, who was that? Yes, our comrade C is a big fellow. He's pretty strong, huh? Yes, he can hoist a lift one-handed. But listen to this: in the war he took out several tanks. He's been decorated. Gee! Then why don't we go to him first, what if I like it there?

Lifts. Cables. Pulleys. What's this, Izrailyevich? She the reinforcements you promised us? Well, it's just that I happen to have an extra half hour today, so... I'm giving the young lady a tour of the factory. We need more workers. A parts manager, maybe—you don't need physical strength for that. As a matter of fact, Kostya, may he rest in peace, only had one arm. But he did just fine... Okay, okay, simmer down now. Do you want to be a parts manager, Tasya? You'll have all these elevators, and lifts, all these neat conveyor belts so you can send out all the components on time? So the devices can be built? What do you say, Tasya? (Her face is tilted up like a little saucer. Her eyes are open very wide. Way up high, where the cable runs through the pulley... all the way up underneath the roof... there's something white up there...) Um, I don't think I can, after all... I'd rather, I think I'd rather do that other thing... be a press operator... Fine. We get it. No, really, it's fine, we'd rather have a regular guy anyway. Cut it out, now; there'll be another batch coming soon. For sure, I promise you.

They get to Twelve. Hello, girls. Here, I'm bringing you a new apprentice. Let me introduce you: Tasya. So here, Tasen-ka, is where we make toys. What we do is we press a sheet of plastic, and presto, we get a little toy gun, all ready to go. The presses are new, it's the most advanced technology. To be sure, it is considered harmful work, press-forming plastic and poly-styrene, by law you aren't allowed to work here yet, but you can start as a batcher or packager. We have fun here. Look, here's our changing room, and that's the shower! And you get milk after your shift. And every so often the labor union gives out free tickets, one time we even saw Lyubchenko herself, can you imagine? So then, you've decided, my dear? I can go? Well, hold on a minute... What's this? You don't want to work here? Oh, please don't be angry! It's just that I still haven't figured it out. Could I look at some more workshops, please?

Goodness, now who'd go being angry with you? Look around and come back to us! Sure, Tasya, let's go have a look around, of course. Just not for too long, I don't have much time.

So what was that?! What's going on?! I don't want to make toys. Get a load of that! What's with you?! What's with these whims?! I want to work at an electronics factory, I don't want to make toys. Well, well, well, Tasenka... Hmm... in that case... we'll head over to the machine shop, then. That's in Nine. But I'm warning you, it's an all-male collective. Nobody's going to coddle you there. You're not afraid of hard work, are you? What about sharpening your cutter, will you be able to do that yourself? Well they'll teach me, won't they, Tasya whispers rapturously. I want to work a machine! And I will! Well I'll be. She's going to work a machine. Fine, let's go.

How-dee-do, Izrailyevich! And what's that you've got there? Tasya!? What kind of a name is that?! That's what they called you in the orphanage? No way, we don't like Tasya. We're gonna promote you to full Anastasiya. One letter for every inch you are tall! Ha-ha-ha! Where are those benches we had around here? Z made some benches, remember? 'Cause she's gonna need two! So what do you think, Tasya? Like it here? That's my girl! Now fellows, you better watch your mouths... and by the way, she's going to be a lathe operator, just like you all. That's what I'm saying. Now look over here, Tasya, here we have comrade K, for example. He also started just like you, back when he was still in school, and now he's up there on the wall of fame every quarter. Show her the kind of parts you make. Gee, they're teeny-weeny! Neat! You like that? You want to make ones like that? I do... but... I just... wait...

Hell's bells. Tasya. What am I waiting for?! I'm not going to get anything done today with you around. That does it, Tasya, I don't know what to do with you. You don't like it here,

you don't want to go there... I don't really like people like you very much, you know? Capricious people. You know what? Seeing as how you came to work, then you don't get to pick where, you just go where you're told. And incidentally you won't get a whole lot in the way of choice here. I'm the one who's just going around coddling you, damned if I know why. That's it, we're going back to Shop Twelve, and basta. Oh... no, no, no, no, no, now don't go doing that, I really just can't stand that, what's with the waterworks...

Greetings, Boris Izrailyevich, what's all this racket over here? Well, see, this little lady came to work at our factory. Her name's Tasya. I'm taking her around, showing her everything. But she's all, I don't want to do this, I don't know how to do that. Hmm. I see. Boris Izrailyevich, you can go back to your office. I'll update you later on the labor assignment for comrade... what's your last name? Comrade M. Now then. Where would you like to work? At an electronics factory, that I understand. What would you like to do? Every day?

I like designing and building things. Designing things? So that means you like tinkering with mechanisms, is that right? Yes... once at the orphanage I even fixed a clock. You fixed a clock? Yes... and I got first place in the model competition with a working model excavator, I thought up a way to build it so that it really would dig, all you had to do was push it a little and then it'd dig for two minutes. It could dig for two minutes? The excavator could really and truly dig? And what did it dig, if it's not a secret? Sand. I'll bring it in and show you, if you want me to. Please could I work in a shop that designs and builds things? Please! Even just as an apprentice, I can do the work, honest I can!

Hmm. Well, here's what I'm going to tell you. We do have a shop like that. It's called the assembly operations shop. What they do there is they put parts together to make subassemblies, then they put those together to make devices. That's this workshop, this one right here. Now hold on a minute, don't celebrate! You need a high-school diploma to work here. Do you understand? And you still have two years to go until then. Three, you say? Mm-hmm. Well, all right. Come on.

Hello, comrades. There's someone I'd like you to meet. This is comrade M. She's going to work with you as an apprentice assembly fitter. That's right, she will be the first young lady in your shop, and so I'm going to ask that, as her comrades, you take her under your wing and treat her with extra sensitivity and loyalty. If the foreman tells me a month from now that you're not up to it, Tasya, you'll go work wherever Boris Izrailyevich sends you. Without a peep. Deal? Deal! Thank you so much, sir! But—what's your name? Have that model excavator in my office first thing tomorrow.

3.

The People's Brigade

Ekaterinhof Park is covered in bright white bird-cherry
blossoms. The petals hang layered in the air, puff up in little powdery heaps, float in lacy rafts down the river, swirl in
the dust. Even after five o'clock the sun still stands above the
warehouses, cranes, and iron roofs. It's spring (sharp, brilliant
smells; breezes; reminders; bird-cherries and fried fish; rank
rot and fresh breezes; the neighborhood's poverty; the clatter-
ing of sharp, rusted roofs), the air is maximally saturated, so
you stop feeling hunger, cold, fatigue, and pain, and all that's
left is a fevered, insomniac receptivity to happiness, an urge to
continually switch activities, flowers, faces; it's the vibrating,
liquid, prismatic air of frenzy. A woman bashes a man in the
head with a piece of rusty pipe, blood pours in a sheet down
his cheeks, and he smiles blissfully. In the housing blocks, the
little eight-year-old daughter of momma Svetka the building
caretaker sits in the entrance and tells scary stories, while her
baby sister Vika squats in her tattered, peeling sandals on the
ground, methodically spitting on the gray asphalt dust and
smearing it around with her finger.

Man! Isn't there a fight somewhere? My hands are itch-
ing, couldn't somebody somewhere just have a good fight today? We should sic the people's brigade on *you*, Pasha! You

should work harder, then you wouldn't have so much extra energy. Guys, I have a plan (pulls a half-liter beaker out of her bag). Whoa there, Tanya, where'd you dig that up? I asked the measurements and standards guys, I told them what it was for and they gave it to me. What's it for? Well *this* is what it's for (tells them). So let's just drop by. I've suspected for a long time now that they've been pouring short. Now Pashka, just where do you think you're going? No, we're not taking you with us anymore. We're keeping things reasonable. You will stay behind and keep a lookout. That's even better: what if there *is* a fight?

Could we have some juice please? (Three glasses of 200 milliliters each. Tanya produces the beaker.) What's that you've got there? Don't worry. We're the people's quality control. (Valya's a detail man, he makes the smallest parts in the whole factory on a lathe so small the workshop nicknamed it "the balalaika.") Now don't you go worrying about anything. The third glassful easily fits in the beaker on top of the first two, and at this point Verrrrka takes center stage. Her voice vibrates threateningly. So. A half-liter beaker! And it all fit! Three 200-milliliter glasses! Call the manager, we are going to officially document our audit. That's right! shout shoppers. We've been seeing this for a long time! Don't give me your "just wait a minute," Verka hammers out. We didn't come here to wait! We came to establish that you are pouring short! And we are establishing it! We don't want anything from you (Valya). Now don't you worry. Everything's going to be okay. But you just can't do that. You see? That's why we're documenting our audit. Because people want to have something to drink. But you pour short. Yes, that's right, everyone says approvingly. That's what we want! But you pour short! We've been noticing this ourselves for a long time now! But if nobody'd come to you with a beaker, you'd've kept right on

pouring short! Those who act with impunity will suffer puni-
tive measures! That's right! Good for these guys.

The saleslady turns sour. (Pashka peeks through the doorway. This is just the right time. Would be the right time. But
Verka is watchful. She brandishes her fist at Pashka. Pashka
promptly assumes an innocent expression: what?)

The four of them walk down the damp, fresh, warm
street. Pashka, is it true that you're a former city boxing
champion? What do *you* think? Everybody knows I am.
And know who my buddy is? A! We were at the same trade
school, we roomed together. How could you not have heard
that? Well, that's just 'cause you're not interested in boxing,
but he's like... he's famous! His fame's resounding everywhere these days. He even took out that world champion,
Savage Hugh; he took him out in the first round. And you
slept in the same room as him? Weren't you afraid? That's
right, we used to jump up in the middle of the night and
spar, and sometimes I even laid him down on his back, no
sweat, lies Pashka. But you just try to get *me* flat on my back!
Verka bristles and puffs up, right in the middle of the street.
She's solidly built, thickset, and her eyes are foreboding,
crazed; she's not joking. Yeah... I'll lay you on your back, no
doubt about it, says Pashka in a way that makes Valya blush
a little, while Tanechka snorts indignantly to herself and ad-
justs her glasses, but Verka doesn't give a rat's ass. Come on,
then! she shouts, and runs at him. Pashka grabs her lazily,
but carefully, in the middle of her dress and throws her over
his shoulder, where she kicks and bucks, playing the game
that's as old as the earth itself... but suddenly Pashka fixates
on something... he tests the air... then he plops Verka back
on the asphalt, not noticing that she's lost a shoe, and races
off. Tanechka: somebody's started a fight. Let's give the guy
a chance to do what he loves best.

Verka (hopping over to her shoe on one foot): hey, wait for me!!

Pashka's already deep in the thick of it. Valya K peers in, but no matter how hard he tries, he just can't figure out who's beating who. And how did Pashka figure it out, off the cuff like that? He didn't figure out a damn thing, he's just hitting whoever his fist lands on, that's all. Valya, hadn't you better go help him? Well isn't that some great advice! Don't go in there, Valya! Girls, I love you so very much, says Valya K. Jeez, I'm trying to look out for you, and you go and smart off. You're just afraid to fight. You abandoned your friend when he was in trouble! Then I'll go in myself! Verrrrka flies over to the fight and grabs one of the fighters by the neck from behind. This surprising dirty trick makes him lose his balance, and he almost falls backward. Verka lets go and jumps away. As she approaches the fight, Tanechka loudly says, "a people's brigade." And this is where it all stops. Not all of it, of course; the commotion goes on for a long time, what with the building caretaker having gotten dragged in, as well as an old shrew with scratched-up legs, and a mom ignoring her many children to pour oil on the flame from her window, but then a Pobeda pulls up and a solid-looking comrade climbs out, and it's not clear who the comrade is, but in the end the conflict is diluted and drains away. Pashka, excited and rumpled but virtually unscathed, is gesticulating and yakking about something. By now the sun is disappearing behind the buildings, and the lindens' gigantic leaves hang almost motionless in the air, and the air smells fresh: there's going to be a storm.

The granny with the scratched-up legs runs, shuffling, after them. Dearies, Komsomol members, help me! My daughter-in-law is sick. Grandma, call a doctor if she's sick. We're a people's brigade. What? A doctor? What doctor!? No doctor can help her. Come with me, I beg you by Christ the Lord, help me… she's young, but she's dying… she's going to die. Don't say Christ the Lord, Valya K retorts, but we'll do it. We'll come and figure out what the problem is.

They follow the granny. We live in a corner, half a room, we got no space, and here I am with two sons, used to be four but my youngest died in the war and the oldest went missing without a trace, and now two live with me, and the younger one, he's like you, he's finishing high school, he's working, but the older one, well he drinks, he got married and he drinks, and now he's made his wife… I don't know how to say it… we got no space, but she wanted a baby so bad, and like he says, she tricked him… so he goes and makes her… you know…

Get an abortion (Verrrrka.)

Yes… and he beat her, and threatened her, and he… well, he broke her spirit… she went and did it… and all she's done since then is lie there, she never eats, she almost never sleeps… she just lies there, no work, no nothing… we had a doctor already, what's the use in doctors… we got a good one, God bless her… she said okay, we'll take her to the psych ward, we can take her, you know, but then, well, you know yourself what that means… and she tells us, you need to bring her out of it as soon as possible… she needs happiness… but where are we going to get that… what kind of happiness can we give her…

The granny frets. The door is open. The ceiling is low, and there's a burnt, damp smell. Had there been a fire? It's dark. A smoky, greasy kitchen, thronging with women in cheap floral-print dresses. A bevy of ragged preschoolers that pushed into the building after the brigade raises a racket in the narrow corridor. The narrow "half-rooms" lie off the corridor. Pashka doesn't go in, he stands in the doorway. The meager square meters are heaped with things, packed with furniture. Hello. We're a people's brigade. Someone brought us…

Why?

Well, we don't know why ourselves.

Leave.

She turns to the wall and pulls the blanket over her head.

Out past the smeared window in its unpainted, dried-out frame, the sleepy, dusty stillness is growing dark. But it's not night: in Leningrad, May brings white nights. No, this is a storm coming in to the Narva Outpost from the sea. At the very last minute before it hits, a yellowish light bursts from low on the horizon, filling the streets.

Out of nowhere, Valya K remembers where and when he saw such a strange light: when he was little and they were leaving Leningrad by barge. Look, Valya's older brother said. Valya turned toward the city and saw above it a fantastical, ominous sun, its glare resounding against the black sky. Mama, is that the end of the world? asked Valya. That was the night the Badayev warehouses burned... and with them most of the city's flour and sugar... on the eve of the 900 days... The barges were being bombed. The one that left before theirs went down with all its passengers.

Verka, her face dark, stares out the window. Pashka has turned back into the gloom of the corridor and is digging in his pocket, extracting the sugar cubes he filched from the factory cafeteria and passing them out to the small fry.

4.

Tanya, Put Me Through

No! No fake exemptions! Are you crazy? You want to land us all in jail? You know we're related to a repressed person!! And you can never forget it, not for a single second! So?! What different times? How are they different? Live as long as I have and you'll see that the times are always the same! Quiet, Lyalya, that's not the point. The point, Tatyana, is that a fake exemption is fraud. We have to observe the law. And the law tells you loud and clear: if you enrolled in night classes, go work during the day. That's the end of it, Tatyana. Do you understand me? And tell your Nadenka, too. I'm not going to go around announcing it, of course, but in my opinion it's dishonest.

So where am I supposed to go find work? In a factory?! Why shouldn't you work in a factory? I don't want to work a machine! I don't want to! And nobody's going to want me at a factory, anyway: I'm a *language and literature* student, see? Get out of here. Get out of here, I said. Look, Lyalya, see what you've taught her. *I* didn't bring you up to be this way! No, I didn't!

And so the next day, there they go down Volynkina, the two friends Tanechka and Nadenka, knocking on all the doors of all the factories' personnel departments. There are six factories on Volynkina. All of them take Nadenka, but none of them take Tanechka. Wait, what? Wait, where? Language and literature? Oh, that's somebody who does the stuff with spelling rules, right? Begging your pardon, but we don't have any vacancies in that area right now. We'll take your friend, but not you. See, I told you so. Nadya, if you like it here, stay! What do you mean?! Without you!?

There it is, the last factory on Volynkina Street, and it's already almost five o'clock. Tanyechka and Nadenka knock shyly on the door of the personnel department. Hello girls, my name's Boris Izrailyevich. And what can we do for you? We enrolled… night classes… I'm in engineering at the polytechnic, my friend's at the university, in language and literature… a philologist… What's that you said, a philologist? Phi-lo-lo-gist… An engineer, that's good. So you're both engineers? No, unfortunately… Tanya here's a philologist… Oh, a philologist! But that's wonderful that you're a philologist, my dear Tanechka. We have us a whole lot of language here at the factory; without a factory education a Russian philologist isn't a philologist at all. Now then, my friends, you probably want to work together, right? Let me just think where to put you… let's see… the production and operations division needs batchers. This is the most necessary and important job in the whole factory, girls. You know what will depend on you? Um… everything! Everything will depend on you! That's why we only allow students to do this job. All our students are either packagers or batchers. Especially philologists. And engineers, too, sure. And then, afterward, they go on to become philologists and engineers. With work experience, though! That's right. Congratulations, girls, as of tomorrow you'll be working in Freedom.

R walks onto the shop floor. She is a woman in full bloom, sultry and tall. Everything about her is big. Enormous breasts.

Bright black hair done up high, like a tower. Dark, prominent eyes. Bright red lipstick. Come with me, dear, R booms. You're the philologist? I will be... Come with me, I need you. (You can't really call R's office an office; it's a glade in the middle of a vast shop floor, set off by potted palms, winding plants wrapped around trellises, monkey-puzzle trees, and calendars.) Repeat after me, dear: MPR2413-R-ZU-58. Tanechka: MPR2413-R-ZU-58. All right. And now: TIU-685-00-R13. Tanechka: TIU-685-00-R13. Now please say something else. It doesn't matter what. *Schlof schein mein voegele* (a hint of surprise in the prominent dark eyes), *mach zu sein oigele?* That's fine. And now, please repeat the first number I gave you. MPR2413-R-58. Not quite. R-ZU-58. Good. Now look here, Tanechka. This is the console. Do you know what a dispatcher's console is? It's the heart of the enterprise. Different sections communicate with each other through the console. Every time someone needs to speak with someone else, he presses a button and asks you to connect him. And you connect him instantaneously. For example, if the factory director needs the director of the assembly shop, you press this button here. And if the production manager has to join the call, then you press here, too. If somebody's not answering over the console, then you just pick up the phone and call him. To do this, you have to know all the factory phone numbers by heart. Moreover, you have to know all the numbers of all the parts that are currently in production. There's something like thirty to fifty of them. For you that's not much, Tanechka. You're a philologist, after all, possessed of a marvelous memory and a quick response time. All you have to do now is develop the professional ability to switch tasks instantaneously. And now here we have someone calling. So we press this button.

Give me H!

Who's H?

Hey, what's with the dispatcher? Where's R?

Not to worry, I'm here. This is my trainee. Trainee! *** the trainee! What the hell's going on over there?! Give me H!

Now you press this over here, Tanechka. H is the deputy chief engineer. Don't worry, dear, you're doing great.

Hey, Tanya, put me through to Y! What about the deadlines? Have you been in to see him? Yes, you got the riot act read to you in full, and rightly so… Ha-ha-ha! Wait, what do you mean, they're redesigning it? Tanya, where's VRP7831-R-PK-8? Still stuck? No, that's not AM-56-U, that's AM-56-E, and the old one, to boot. Because you've got to do your *** job, that's why! Put me through to Thirteen, whoever's there today! Sonya, are you going on lunch soon? He's just ***!! I'd like to know what the hold-up is with STD587-O-19. Dima, man, you didn't forget anything, did you? He's off to Moscow tomorrow. Not hiding any underused communists under the counter, are you? He was ordered to be there immediately. How many in English and how many in Russian? At four-thirty we're getting started on the Globe. Let them know about that adjusted deadline! What do you mean, he left?! We're all flying out to Severodvinsk as an official group on the seventeenth, tickets will be ready for pick-up tomorrow. They didn't distribute anything. Put me through to U! Tanya, give me T. Why is C keeping quiet over there? Tanechka, where's AKS-547-L-2117 right now? Any way we've got it on hand? Well that just means I've got to get through! What the ***, that's ***! Our entire production plan's derailed, and you're going to sit here and give me excuses!! Ah, *** him, he's ***, and he's been *** the entire quarter! ***! Sorry, Tanechka! Any chance you need to step out to the Komsomol office for fifteen minutes or so? I'm going to yell something fierce. Oh, you can't leave the console? Then cover those little ears, please…

Wine, cake, and flowers on the table. R: Tanechka, now you've got your degree, you're a philologist, you can leave our Freedom and go wherever you wish. I'm also leaving, actually. Yes, it's true. Because my husband's relatives emigrated to Israel. Yes, but that's just the rules, girls. Why, because I work here… I could leak something, is the thing. Now, Tanechka, you're free of Freedom, you can go teach children in school. You can become a writer or journalist. You can take up archeology or aviation design. Have children. I don't even know what all you can go do now. But if you decide to stay at our Freedom, then I'll know what kind of person is taking my place. Wait. You'll make a marvelous chief dispatcher. Wait! If you reconsider, tell me right away. You've got twenty-four hours. Oh, yes, by the way, some young man from accounting stopped by, he was looking for you… I don't know his name… Tanya, where are you going?

5.

The Factory
Agitational-Propaganda Troupe

My mama was a film developer at the Leningrad Film Studio.
Papa was an operetta performer. I grew up backstage. When
I was little I was always asking my parents to take me onstage. Onstage!? they'd say. Papa'd say, not a chance, you'll
go wacko on us. Mama'd say, one of these wise-guys here'll
lead you astray. So I marched on over to the regional executive
committee, straight to the director of youth job placement: I
want to work in a factory, and that's final! Mama's in Lenfilm
and papa's in theater, so I want to work in a factory! Of course
my parents started pulling their hair out... mama goes, oh my
god, says mama, but that's the dregs of society, after all! We're
the dregs of society, Verka! *I'm* society's dregs!? According to
my mama, we're the dregs. Water under the bridge now, too
late to change it, my folks had to deal with it... Well it's better to
flaunt a screwdriver than flap your tongue! What's that you're
singing, what's that from? It's from here (holds up a bottle). I
grab this by the neck and the song pours out my throat! Can
you sing that one song, the one from that movie, what was it
called... If you tell me what movie it was... Girls, time to get
some sleep, we're heading out tomorrow. Wait, where? Pinduby. Get a load of that! All the way to Pin-doo-bee! Now that's

the sticks! Look out everybody, they're headed to Pinduby. What? What are you looking at us like that for? What's the deal with Pinduby, anyway? Don't let 'em get to you. They're just trying to get us all riled up. No, really, just go on and tell us, right now, so we know what the deal is with Pinduby. Well, there's... there's nothing wrong with it, really... it's just that... well... So listen, do you all have some guys going with you? No, Marik doesn't count. Marik, you know we have nothing but the utmost respect for you. But... you understand. So do you have any real guys? Because ten to one there'll be a fight. You know what they're like out in Pinduby... Basically all those little tiny villages're full of thugs. You know what they did to their district Party secretary one time...? No use trying to scare us. As soon as we start singing, they'll... Ten to one you won't even get out of here anyway. I go tell my granny to turn on the rain all night, and you don't get out of here tomorrow. Wash the road right out, nothing to it. What's the matter? You don't like it here? We got you your pork, and look, you'll each get you your pail of milk... Damn straight, we're living pretty good these days, but the only thing is you can't leave us. No how, no way. All hail the alliance of the city and the village! We want us a *real close* alliance, don't we, Verka? What granny? What're you flapping your tongue about? Tell them, Platon: can she do it? His granny? She sure can! That granny of his can do anything! Whatever she wants! Kachurov himself goes to see her, asks her to do things. She can turn the rain on, turn it off... So what kind of meteorological management methods does she use? Hmm? Well, I don't know, she's got some kind. She whispers something, and dances around a little. Nonscientific methods, that's what kind. The moment you set foot on Soviet territory all nonscientific methods cease to be in effect. Well, but my granny's a relic of the past, her political consciousness isn't developed yet. Try as you might, she'll keep on with her whispering and dancing, and what do you know... Don't go overboard trying to scare us, now. Next you're gonna tell us you're a wizard yourself. Me?! Of course I'm a wizard! I'm an accordionist! What did you expect? Hey Marik, let's have us a little squeeze-box competition: who can out-squeeze the other? Whoa, none of that! It's loud enough when just one of you plays! Hey, Seryoga, that's enough, we still have to get out to Pinduby tomorrow. Listen, out at that factory of yours, do you have anything that... jiggles? Like riding on a tractor...? Come on, Alyona, quit putting the moves on him. Shame on you. And shit, tuck those shameless tits of yours back in... Can't you just sit there like a normal person... Who, me? *I'm* the one putting the moves on?! What is this, can I not just ask a simple question!? Don't be so jealous!! Alyona, now don't piss me off. It's very simple with me. All I have to do is... Stop it! Get him off! Somebody get him off! Yup, that's what I was always afraid was gonna happen. Marik, enough with the music already! Put the damn bandura down. Can't you see this isn't a good time?! I'm just providing the accompaniment, comrades... A-company-ment, huh?! Now that's some company-ment!! We do them up right, a whole suckling pig, and this is how they repay us?! They start sniffing around our girls, is that it?! Take it easy, these folks came out here to play and sing for us, they're guests... and by the way, they're working people too... So what was that all about, did he want to show us what it's going to be like in Pinduby? He's always like that in the spring, don't pay any attention to him. You're a freaky bunch out here, guys. Granny's a witch... accordionist's flailing and flapping like a... a bat... A bat? What makes you say that? We're field laborers, we work out in the open, in the sunshine... not like the ones who work in the woods... those foresty types, they're strange ones... life is tough, the collective farm's poor, nothin' but cranberries. And bogs. But with us everything's for real! The real deal! Yeah, the real deal, Valechka, not like you churning out that crap on your balalaika. You—!! What about you, Verochka, always on me, always trying to get my goat!! Okay, folks, that's enough! Let's go! We still have to get to Pinduby! But we've only got a couple hours to sleep before it's time to go. Okay, guys, I won't take it personally. Nobody's taking anything personally. Everything's okay. Everything's okay. Me and you, you and us, see, everything's all right. Everything's going swell... just swell... Okay! Everything's all right! Verka, don't be mad! I'm just a simple sailor man... me and you and we... and how's that go... nothin' but cranberries...

6.

Director G. Intermedio.

The first director of the Freedom Factory? Nobody knows anything about him. Nothing on the Internet, either? Well, there you have it. I don't know a single thing about him, except that his name was G. But you can't write that down, because the names of people associated with the factory have to be encoded in Latin letters. Preferably, a single Latin letter. And so for us he's going to be just G. We have his signature on lots of documents from the fifties. See, this signature here. You could always try to read these chicken scratches and figure it out, but I don't see any point in doing that. You know what I think? If you ain't got something, then that's a thing you ain't got. No use trying to force it, drag some meaning out of it. So there was this guy, this Director G. On paper. But maybe he never really existed at all. Whoever knew him personally would've either died or left the factory ages ago. Died, most likely. But maybe nobody did know him personally. How he died? There's kind of a legend about that. People say he was shoveling show off the roof of the main building and fell off the Central Tower. You know, an accident. But some say it wasn't an accident. You could try asking W for more details.

Of course I've seen G, he used to go around the workshops all the time. What he was like? A production worker.

Maybe as a director he wasn't as great as N, who replaced him. But basically everybody was okay with him, and that's why he was appointed. It's true he did drink a lot, but who cares, as long as it didn't affect his work. As a director he was very problematic for the ministry, but he was appointed because he was a good production worker. He was constantly at loggerheads with the bosses and had a lot of problems as a result. Including psychological problems. But anyway, if you want to know about G you should go talk to YY. I should add that he doesn't work at the factory now, but I'll give you his number. He used to talk to G a lot, that I remember for sure. Me? I was very young back then. For me the director was a giant among men!

Well no, that's all a bunch of crap. G never went around the factory. Not like our N, he'd always be scouring the shops. That guy, he was the one who knew everybody. But G was appointed from above, he was a typical apparatchik. Didn't know the first thing about production. He was just a conformist. A real Party-line conformist. He was appointed way back under Stalin, and he stole everything that wasn't nailed down. He just went through the motions of being director. And he was a horrific drunk, too. The only reason he wasn't removed was because he was some big-wig's little boy. And then what happened, he fell off the roof, that's right, landed in the middle of the courtyard. What snow?! He was just drunk. No idea what could've made him go all the way up there. But some people even say it was actually murder. That they'd decided to just get rid of him already and give the factory a competent director. Personally? No, that's also crap. I did not know him personally, and I actually never even spoke with him, not once. He didn't know the first thing about production. But his deputy is another story, I talked with his deputy all the time. His deputy was a really interesting guy. Looked a lot like G, wonder how on earth he managed to find him. But he was a completely different person. Outwardly he looked like G, but he was completely different. Yeah. You know, you'd be better off asking... listen, there is one lady, last name of J. Did W tell you about her? I see. Bellochka, I'm sorry for interrupting you, would you happen to have J's phone number? Yes, I've got a pen...

Oh my goodness, G, yes, we did know each other a little! An erudite engineer and a marvelous conversationalist... he spoke English well. Refined manners. He was a little modest, a little closed, of course, but he was so straightforward! He dressed elegantly. He knew wine. I remember, once he... or no, wait, that wasn't G, that was... yes... that was my second husband... Well, you see, I was, you might say I was friends with him, but now it's been so long that I can't really say anything for certain anymore, except that he was just the most kind and pleasant person... Yes, unfortunately, he did die young... It was his own deputy director, a man he trusted implicitly... seems to have been an accident... something like they got into a fight up there... I don't know for sure, it's an awful story... I think he was hoping to take his place, that simple. There was a court case afterwards, very public, you know, but then they went and acquitted him, they said it was the effect of his condition, or something like that... Why, but there's nothing to thank me for, I didn't help you at all!

G? He lived at the factory. I mean, he didn't even leave at night. He had an apartment, but he didn't live there. No need for him to live there anyway... he was single. Unsociable. A little awkward. And of course the times... so to speak... you know what I mean... he'd been running the factory since back in Stalin's day. You don't fulfill the production plan, you get shot. So in that case you kind of can't help but... No, no, there was no actual roof involved, he just meant that G was

so stressed out, had so many problems, that he could easily have... you know... I mean, of course he was getting treatment for it, that's one detail that I remember for sure. I mean, he was a regular guy overall, but every once in a while it'd just come over him, this trauma from being wounded in the war, he'd survived some horrible event he never talked about. It was something that was so... when he was in an inebriated condition, as they say, he'd talk about it, but I don't know for sure what he said, so I'm not going to make things up... I mean, it's not worth it, anyway, if afterward the guy doesn't even remember what he said. G also had this deputy, or rather, it wasn't a deputy, it was him, but a totally different person. It's hard to understand if you haven't seen it yourself. But I wasn't close to him, I didn't know him directly... Hey, you know who really knew G well is—just don't say this person's name, he hasn't had any ties to the factory for years. So don't you say who he is, don't even give a letter...

G was honest to a fault. That's something I can say for sure. And he was unquestionably brave. Foolhardy, even. He was wounded many times in the war. Took so much fire... probably looked like swiss cheese... And then this is quite a story, the time he... Turn off your dictaphone [...]

What G did after the war? Nothing. Not a thing. He couldn't. And along comes the deputy director of the city executive committee, who'd worked with him before the war, and finds him in a pretty poor state. So he makes him director of the factory. Hoped that'd make him perk back up, kind of come back to life. But it was too late. I mean, so in what sense too late—it wasn't too late for the factory. G was fine as a director. Back then our subcontractors weren't so hot. You know how people say that N, wow, he was a great director, a genius, and all the rest of it, but G, like, couldn't get anything done, didn't have the drive. But none of that's right—it's not fair.

It's just that Freedom's time still hadn't come. Back when G was here, they were still putting all their resources into aviation. They thought we'd catch up to the Americans in the air. But once they realized we'd never catch up to anybody in the air, then they started funneling everything into submarines. And that's when N got here, and everything just started moving. Some big story! And G, he just kind of landed right in the break between shifts. Between epochs. But as a person he was no worse than N. I knew them both well, you can trust me on that. Except that N, he was a Communist, no matter what. He was a clear-headed, straightforward person. A force. Whereas G was a person divided. In the real sense. No, I'm not going to explain anything. No, he didn't get any treatment for it, because he knew if he remembered everything, he wouldn't be able to go on living. That is, he did remember. Once. And – you know what happened. By the way, he was the one who renovated the factory. He had gravel spread over the grounds between the buildings. He fixed up the workshops, brought in machine tools. Shop Four was even built under him, back in 1957.

About his drinking? Fairy tales. This is what I'll tell you about his drinking: G was a dyed-in-the-wool teetotaler. One hundred percent. Don't you believe anybody who says he drank. G never touched a drop of the hard stuff. He was never drunk.

7.

The Lily

On the thirteenth of December, the brand-new director, N—he was a great man, two months in and he already knew everyone in the factory by name—N comes into our shop and he says, I know it's impossible to finish four Lily data link targeting systems for our Yak-28L tactical bombers by New Year's. That said, what'll it take for you to get them done?

It's a new day here at Freedom. The factory's hiring anybody who graduated from a vocational school, hiring them by the hundreds. It's bringing in equipment from Japan, building dorms, mobilizing everyone and everything. World War Three seems imminent.

One lead man steps forward: first of all, 299 rubles a month. (Three hundred's not allowed.) Done, says N.

Another one steps forward: put some cots in here, then, so we don't have to leave. Consider them here already, N says. And there always has to be a full carafe of hooch right here. Not watered down! Deal, says N. We'll make sure of it. Is that all? That's all, they say. And they make four Lilies by New Year's.

It goes without saying that these aren't exactly the finest Lilies ever grown. The way A put it is—A's the head of Shop Twenty, finishing and delivery—as A likes to say, they're the kind you'll still have to "fucking fuck with" to get them to work. But right now, nobody cares. Everyone's in a holiday frame of mind.

Then along comes summer, and it hits the fan. It becomes evident that the device doesn't meet some of the specs. A lot of them. However, this only becomes evident once they start installing the Lily in the planes. So the finishers from Twenty fly out to Irkutsk to finish the Lily on the go, so the bombers can do their job. This whole big serious rapid-response team flies out to install a Lily that's still completely raw, that our very own Freedom Factory had developed while they were three sheets to the wind in just two weeks.

The team gets there and sees it can't do a damn thing.

Everything's a mess, everything's raw. The Lily is completely raw, it isn't finished yet. Parts of it were even slapped together any which way. Have to admit that the aircraft themselves weren't any better. All their equipment was also raw. Including everything the Lily needed, everything it worked in sync with. Pray tell, just how are we to go about, oh, for example, reaching the ground radio relays back on the home front, when the on-board radio set has no jamming blockers? Too late to fix it. But everyone was happy they'd found somebody to blame. Everyone had been working three sheets to the wind, obviously, everyone had been cutting corners to get it done by New Year's. So then, naturally, everyone pushed back, made excuses... everyone except Freedom, that is. So the military reps really laid into the finishers from Freedom. They said, what do you think you're doing here, you lazy bums? What'd they bring you out here for? Can you do anything, anything at all, to get this piece of crap to work? Even a little bit? Our inspection's in ten days! So whaddaya got? How are we supposed to conduct targeted bombing in adverse weather conditions? You were bragging that with your

Lily, we could get a CEP of 50 meters on the target, but now you can't even establish a decent connection to the ground stations! Heads are gonna roll!

The finishers mumble their completely valid justifications. The plane itself hasn't even gone through a full round of flight tests, they say. There's still time, they say. And meanwhile, what about the military-industrial inspection committee? It's already on its way. There's going to be a gigantic meeting in Irkutsk. The Minister's coming, and the chairman of the Regional Economic Council, and factory directors... and it's not just the Lily, there's a whole slew of other issues, too! And then N arrives. And all the Party bigwigs, and the whole committee, and the regional Party committee's defense division—they all saw the lay of the land, so they ganged up on Director N and pinned all the blame on him. They raked him over the coals because of the hooch, and because of the 299-ruble salary, and they even blamed him for the subcontractors' shoddy work, too. So we all start thinking, looks like our dear director's getting the boot, but we know he's not gonna go without taking us down too, we'll be the ones held responsible, we'll get the blame: it was the finishers, they're the ones who couldn't knock the thing into shape. Now we're all going to be fired on the spot! We'll be drawn and quartered!

But N wasn't out to draw or quarter anybody. He says, listen. You know I was director of another factory entirely during the war. We made the partisans' radio equipment. That you know. But afterwards, I did time. That you don't know. I was sentenced in the Leningrad case and sent up north to cut timber. Then I was rehabilitated. Completely. I'm telling you this so you know I'm not afraid. And also so you know I don't have any issues with you. I can see how it all turned out this way. Now. They gave us a deadline for fixing everything. But first we all need to take a break. Otherwise we won't be able to work. And that's why we're all leaving tomorrow for an obligatory vacation on the Baikal. Camping. I'll get the transportation and grub taken care of.

That just blew our minds. Nobody in their wildest dreams could've thought that a factory director would do something like that in a situation like this! We still hadn't gotten to know our N.

N really did convince the director of the Irkutsk Airplane Plant to give us a bus. We went out to the Baikal and set up our tents. Forty or so of us went. For three days we did nothing but eat, drink, and relax. And only then, after that, was it: how are we going to get out of this?

And even then, N didn't utter a single word of blame, he didn't criticize a single person. Not even the ones who deserved it. We sat down, nice and easy, and talked about it half the night, then made our decision in nothing flat. Each of us knew what he personally was supposed to do. We got back in the morning and each of us went to do his job, and we got to work, nice and easy. We got it all done and turned in on time. It seemed like a miracle. And it was a miracle.

In all, one hundred and eleven Yak-28L bombers were outfitted with the Lily. The aircraft was given the NATO reporting name Brewer-A.

8.

Antarctica

It doesn't look like such a long street, our Volynkina, but there's no fewer than six enterprises on it. And all of them get rolling first thing in the morning: Mettrans, LEMZ Precision Instruments, the Kapelsky, the chocolate factory, and the prototype production plant for Science and Research Institute № 4, a little off to the side. And last but not least: Freedom. The street gets mobbed! By seven, even by six forty-five, if you please. Director N goes around scouring the shops and boy, he sees everything. Late? Here's your fine. Skipping work? Here's your written reprimand. By the time N came to Freedom, there were a lot of people there, and even more work. Some jobs ran three shifts.

The lunch lines are horrendous. All the workshops break for lunch in shifts. Some of them don't have time to eat: as soon as you get your meat patty, the whistle blows, so stuff it in your gob and off you trot.

And who do we have here? It's none other than comrade F, still just a whippersnapper. Today F hasn't even gone to the cafeteria. Instead of going to lunch, he's going to the head of his workshop and announcing, I'm quitting. I'm headed to Antarctica.

What? Where? To Antarctica. There's work for me. My buddy told me. They need technicians, so I'm going. I'll service equipment. Here are my workplace leaving papers; sign them, please. Now wait just a minute, F. Come on. Stop this. What is there to wait for, Valery Nikiforovich? They're asking, so I'm going... I'm just supposed to let you go, then? Well, hell. Leningrad not exciting enough for you? Fine. Come see me tomorrow.

Radio-Nanny is our watering hole. Go down the right side of Volynkina and it's there just before you hit Strike Prospect. That's not its official name, of course. It's called that because it's right next to the section of the Kirov department store that sells record albums and radio parts, and also, yeah, because the radioelectronics finishers from Freedom drink there. Not much to it: little tables, some nibbles. It's dark inside. Hey, F, how's it going? What's new? (They expect me to start entertaining them.) To Antarctica? Ha-ha-ha! No, I'm—I really am. I already got my leaving papers. Hear that? He really is! You're nuts, F. What's the big deal? Antarctica's the Soviet Union. Do what?! Yeah, we were the first to discover it. Our man. What was his name... Fyodor Fyodorovich Amundsen. Don't get all bent outta shape, buddy. You two just butted heads; he's a little ornery, you're a little ornery... No, fellas. I'm going. I'll be out there among the icy floes and hummocks, releasing a meteorological probe. Know what that is? Right, it's this great big balloon. One guy was reeling one out, reeling it out slow, and he up and flies away himself. Five kilometers up it stops, and he's just hanging there. How'd they get him down? They didn't. He bought the farm, poor stiff. Get outta here! No, that's what happened, for sure. Antarctica's no joke, brother. A hundred below zero, Celsius. Well then... hey, listen! When you sail past America, say hi for us. But wait a minute, F, what about Lyuba? What about her? Well, you won't be back for a year! So she'll wait. And if she doesn't, then... then she doesn't. No way, F, you've gone off it for sure! Give up a girl like that for some polar bears? Polar bears live in the Arctic, idiot. Antarctica's the opposite... How's it opposite!? It's got teddy bears. Man! Don't go anywhere, F, at least you're fun! (I'm fun for these people. But somehow you're no fun for me, folks... I can't do a damn thing right in this life.) Ah, lay off, kids. A year's not that long. But is B even going to let you go? Heck, he'll be more than happy to see the back of me!

Lunchtime comes again the next day. F stands there, papers in hand. Go see the director. Go see him right now. Is he going to try to get me to stay? I haven't a clue.

So what's the story, comrade F? Leaving? Giving up in the face of hardship, are we? What do you mean, giving up... quite the opposite. In Antarctica they need technicians... radar technicians... But how's that hair of yours gotten so long? Here's twenty kopecks, go on over there across the street and get a haircut. And come see me tomorrow. Same time. Yury Mikhailovich, I can't! My leaving papers... What's that? He can't, he says?! Get out of here, now! Tomorrow I want you right here! With your hair cut! I don't need twenty kopecks, I've got it. See you tomorrow.

...but aside from Radio-Nanny, there's also a beer kiosk. A little further down Kalinkina Street, on the corner of Kalinkina and Rakhmetov. It's called the Three Streams, because there's always three streams flowing there: beer, water, and... urine. The kiosk's manned by Anatoly. War veteran, one arm. Hi. And why is our F so jolly, with a brand-new haircut to boot? The director made me. That N of ours, keeps us all trimmed. Yeah, um, I'm going to Antarctica. Well, well. To Antarctica? I'm serious. Okay, cut him off.

So where else can you get a drink? You can get a drink on the riverbank in Ekaterinhof Park. You can actually swim there, but not now. It's April now. All the timber in Ekaterinhof Park was sent down the river back before the war. And after

the war F's brother drowned here. They were skating and he fell through the ice. There were people around, and they did run for help, but he drowned. So now F sometimes has a drink on the bank of the Ekaterinhof River. Sort of in memory of his brother. Although he remembers him just fine without it. His brother was a year older and exactly the same as F, except much better. That's how it always goes. The best ones drown. The not-so-great ones drudge their lives away. The more he drinks, the stronger it comes washing over him. You wouldn't say F was drunk just looking at him; he was behaving. Whistling and shouting erupts at the Kirovets stadium. Freedom is playing the Kirov factory. F also plays soccer, true, but he's on the B-team. Little boys sit under the bleachers, or in the tree, there's a great big linden there... They sit and watch. No, he's not on the A-team, that's out of his league, as they say... you need perseverance. But F's got no perseverance for that. You also need discipline. And strength of character. (F gathers a pile of dry leaves under himself and scratches a match alight.) There we are. (Smoke.) And Lyuba? What about Lyuba. It don't mean a thing to her, as they say. You just think that. Didn't you go and get her knocked up? I don't know. And I don't care. Find out first. What if they don't let you go? If they don't let me go, I'll go anyway. To hell with it. To hell with it all.

Mm-hmm. You got a haircut. Good. Now on to business. I'm not letting you go. You have to let me go, no matter what. Antarctica. You need money? Is that it? We can figure something out. Give you a raise. No, that's not it, Yury Mikhaylovich. So what's the problem? Ah, you and German must've had it out again. I heard about you two. Knuckleheads, the both of you! I know he's right. I do. It's just... that's the way I am. I thought I'd be different here, with you all, but I'm the same way here, too. It's the same old story. So you think Antarctica's going to change you, right? Well, I don't. Yeah... I don't either. You don't? Then why are you leaving? Well?

Fine, Yury Mikhaylovich. I get it. You're not letting me go. No means no. Goodbye.

Stop! Where do you think you're going, F? I'm not finished with you yet! Now you just sit yourself on down. That's right. Get yourself a piece of paper, my friend. Just like that. And write. Good. Write, I pledge that every day for the next three months I will... Good. I don't have to see you myself, you'll sign in with my secretary. Although if you do get the urge to have a little talk, I'll see you. Good. Keep writing. If I do not perform these duties... yes, F, write it just like that! "Despicable!" And in the event of your death during these three months, we will carve on your tombstone that you're despicable! Three months from now, on July fifteenth, we are meeting right here in my office! Sign it! Geared up for Antarctica, he was! Some polar explorer!

9.

Inga and the Women of Hell

The women in the hot-dip galvanizing shop sail along in mighty canvas smocks tarred with streaks, fumes and shadows and dotted with holes drilled by drops of acid. Plunge them in boiling water and remove the skins. G pinches a small iron key between his thumb and index finger and swings it around and around in circles. Somehow you're just unhappy with everybody, ladies, you are always unhappy with everybody. I can't figure you out. I mean I, personally, I just *can not* figure you out. Maybe it's because I'm not married. Nah, that wouldn't help you. You think not? You? Not a chance. A fog hangs under the white rusted ceiling. The air blooms with greenish flakes and showers, with cabbagey mold and vapor. The suggestion of working over the weekend is met with no enthusiasm. My left slipper's ripped, now it takes in water over the side, like a boat. If I was floating in it, I wouldn't get five meters before it went under. Good thing I'm not floating in it. Thin-soled cardboard slippers, the heels long ago worn down unevenly. Unevenness means you're frivolous. That's right, Manechka, you are a frivolous young lady. You must be joking, right? Where do you think we're going on a Saturday? (She looks in her pocket mirror, locks her lips up tight with two more passes of the lipstick.) Our neighbors in the communal apartment gnaw their sugar loaf every evening. You think she doesn't want something sweet too? She loafs around in the hallway all day, but they won't take her in the nursery school, she's got these little sores on her head—but I'm not taking her in there anyway, the kids'd tease her to death. If she'd been in a nursery school, she'd've started talking ages ago. Katya, but were those really men, though? They gave you nothing but tears, nothing but tears. As long as you're here, Pavel Arkadyevich, I'll just take this opportunity to tell you: we don't have time to eat lunch. And our production process here is harmful enough as it is. Yeah, you know I stop by to visit you ladies, but I mean it's like the fires of hell in here. Helen here, Helen there, what Helen, if you're not going to, you know, you could at least—but instead you just... (The green fog parts briefly under the oily yellow heat of the ceiling lamp.) Thank you kindly for that, of course, but to be honest, how many times can you really say thank you? Now I would say thank you if there was hot water on our floor in the dorm. In the winter we danced out to the trolleybus, but the trolleybus was packed... No, I don't need any tights, could you distribute tickets to something instead, maybe like to the Operetta Theater. But I can't come in on Saturday, I didn't know, see, I could've told my mama and she'd have come out, but now she can't get here in time. Hey, Katya, don't worry, I can't either. And basically I mean wait a minute, what is this they're starting to pull on us now... But that's nothing compared to the day before yesterday... there went Frida, running as fast as she could... Oh, you were there too? Yeah. Eighteen parts down the drain. What? But that wasn't on us, they were the ones specified the wrong surface, we did pickle them but it wasn't the right place. There, feast your eyes on that, a real beauty. No, I'm not going in on a Saturday, not a chance. I'm reading this really interesting book right now, some young doctor wrote it, there's these Kegel exercises in there, they help you become a real woman. I'm already a real woman. He took a bulb syringe and... I was so horrified that I ran off and had the baby. No way, I'd never be willing to do that, too scary. Yes they do, too, my friend from school is married to a powder monkey and they get whole packs of them, hundreds of them, want to know why? Because if they portion out the charges into condoms first, then it's easy to lay them, and they don't get wet in the trench. Well but do you have kids, Pavel Arkadyevich? There, you see! Plus the weather's supposed to be nice on Saturday.

If you look out the window, you can see the profile of a huge girl on top of the asphalt. It's made of the cracks in the asphalt that was laid over the concrete slabs. And there's another concrete slab in the girl's head. A girl with a slab. Beats your "girl with an oar" any day. The profile isn't of a very young girl, and it's not all that good a profile, either. Her cheek's sprinkled with something wet and green. And now the girls in the anodizing brigade—the one where they dip parts in a sulfuric acid anodizing bath, hold them there, and then take them out again—have twelve baths instead of six. And while it used to be that you'd only get acid on your skin if you were being careless, now you have to pull every part up out of the acid and run around with it from one bath to another, so the acid... well... basically it is what it is, we've just had to get used to it. Recently Galina Semyonovna took a dive right in the middle of the shop floor. No big deal. So yeah, she falls down, and yeah, she lays there for a little while, then she gets up and gets back to work. To tell the truth it's all because the metal floor's so slippery. It's actually kind of hard to work like that. And nobody has the slightest desire to be here on a Saturday, and seems to me it's not that hard to see where they're coming from on that. You can see where we're coming from, right, Inga Alekseyevna? I can see where you're coming from. (Inga, a lawyer, has never worked at a galvanizing bath. She grew up in a two-room apartment with a piano and books all the way up to the ceiling. And the ceilings were four meters high. She's a lawyer. She dresses in elegant angles and shadows. A small, graceful, stern woman with a soft voice.) It doesn't comply with the labor code. We'll get the labor union involved if we need to. Oh, give me a break! You'll get *Pal Arkadyich* involved? But he's... No, but she's... I'm telling you, don't get all these men tangled up in this. Manechka. Inga Alekseyevna, give me a break! Anything but that, please! We weren't trying to... That's not what we meant. No, no, no, listen, it's just like they say: you can get away with anything, once... But they're going to fine you. No, absolutely not, this issue definitely has to be raised, and I won't name any names. Ah, Inga Alekseyevna, you're still so young, you don't know them yet. But they know you. They know you.

Hello, Inga, hello... Yes, come in, of course you can come in... No, I don't know anything. Right. Of course the comrades have complained about you. So this form here, I think this is from you, right? The issue here is that we need to fulfill the plan. No, be quiet, Inga. The issue is that we need to fulfill the plan. And this order form here is where it's all laid out, plain and simple. Well, I think it's not quite so plain and simple after all, from what they were... So what were they saying? Well, they were saying things. And what about overtime? If there's an urgent need, then... Yeah, yeah, what urgent need. There's no urgent need. You listen to them all you want. But what happened is that they blew their deadline. They're the ones who blew their plan fulfillment deadline, don't you see? So now it's who's to blame? Who's guilty? The galvanizers? No, they just pin everything on them. Because the women don't make a peep, the women dutifully... And

they did say something, keep that in mind! Children, Saturday, Sunday. There's nobody to leave the children with! Why should they have to come in on Saturday to their hellish work, where in hellish conditions they… no, *you* wait! Why is the floor slippery in there? What, is there no such thing as putting down floorboards? Why is Nine being renovated, when it was just renovated seven years ago, while in Thirteen a veteran of labor is falling down in the middle of her shift? What are you waiting for, you want somebody to dissolve?! What are you going to bury then?! Acid?! You go choke on it!!

Inga. Inga! Okay. (A silence that can't be called anything other than: a prolonged silence.) So now tell me this. Did the entire shop refuse to come in, or did some of them go ahead and come in? Aha, so that means that at least some did… Now you just wait a minute!! That's not what I'm getting at!! You know what? You know how we're going to do this? We're going to do this from the other direction. We won't withhold the plan fulfillment award from whoever didn't come in. But we will give bonuses to the ones who did. Can you live with that? Good. And now about the rest of it. I agree with you. The thing with the floorboards is an ongoing problem. But it's just that I got a promise that next quarter there'll be… look, I went to Moscow with B and we managed to wangle some new equipment, so now they'll have it a little easier. But it makes no sense to put down floorboards before then, because we'll have to rearrange everything anyway. Can they wait for one more quarter? Inga, you're doing a great job, and that's a fact. No, I am not going to go and have a talk with him, either, it's just that he doesn't always think through all the consequences, he's set in his ways, he's got his own limitations. And how are they supposed to know the laws? That's what we've got you for. Go on, Inga, they'll get their floorboards tomorrow. Hello! Yes, if he's already here then send him in!

10.

Engineer H

So N, our new director, comes here from the other factory he used to run and brings H with him as his new chief engineer. H turned out to be a real strange one. Looked nothing like a factory type, just a spindly intellectual. Young, but basically bald already. Only a few sparse remnants of hair sprouting around the sides of his head. Quiet voice. Big eyes, perfectly gray. And here's the thing: over there at that other factory, he'd been in charge of the Experimental Design Bureau, not the actual factory itself. And then everybody goes oh, right, we get him now. Nobody's arguing, it's perfectly clear that he's a super smart guy. A design engineer. That kind of thing. But see, a factory is another matter altogether. Managing a factory and managing an EDB are two very distinct differences. The chief engineer of a factory isn't just responsible for all the technical drawings and suchlike, he also has to take care of it when one of the guys goes on a bender, or can't get his bike to stay up, or whatever. And what we've got here, brother, is... that's right, what we've got here is a factory. We've got us a real... but he's all spindly, this H. And everybody concludes that H is probably not gonna make it in Freedom.

So then our certified finishing technicians, many of them with university degrees, they put their heads together and

they decide, this is what we're going to do. We've been working with this device here for many years, we know it inside
and out. We're going to give H a little off-schedule test, one
there's no way he can pass. That's not very nice! intervened
the most scrupulous among them. He still has to work here,
but nobody'll respect him after that. No, the first ones coun-
tered, we're not going to haul off and, you know, let him have
it right off the bat, we just want to see how the guy handles
himself in a difficult situation. How he'll get out of it. Where
he goes for help, who he turns to, or whether he just acts like
that's the way it's supposed to be. Basically we're just feeling
him out.

So that's what they do, they give him a little test. They
took the device they were calibrating and broke certain
things inside it, broke them very cleverly, so that the device
ended up with two unrelated defects. And then they act like
they've been working on it for days, trying to figure out
what's wrong. So in comes H, takes one look at the thing with
those gray eyes of his and just offhand he goes, here's where
A, B, and C aren't working, you need to do X, Y, and Z to fix
it. And then he goes quiet for a minute, and then he adds,
musingly, there's just one thing I can't understand, which
is how all this could've happened at the same time. Because
it couldn't have. A bewildering, intriguing case. And off he
goes. And the highly qualified finishers just watch him go,
and then one of them says, but how? How did he know? And
another one adds, people are saying that N only agreed to
switch over to our factory once they promised to give him H.
Otherwise he wouldn't switch, not a chance. (And that really
is the way it was.)

Later, after H had been accepted, after people had gotten
used to him and acclimated to his ways, everyone saw that he
was, as the factory's Chief Dispatcher M put it, just darling.

Even-tempered, often melancholy, H never raised his voice. In this he was the diametric opposite of the loud-mouthed, big-bellied head of the finishing shop, B, Director N's other protégé and appointee. B never talked when he could yell. You could say that the two of them, B and H, represented the opposite poles of human nature, the two ends of the rainbow, the two antithetical Kretschmer types. Chief Engineer H drank absolutely nothing (a hundred grams of vodka on holidays, which lent H's drawn cheeks a ruddy glow and curved his thin lips in an involuntary, urbane smirk), while B tossed back buckets of vodka, sometimes to the point of choking, and would miss work for weeks at a time (the written reprimands came raining down, which for managers at his level is really overkill). H spoke clearly, quietly, and little, mostly remaining silent, while B was incapable of shutting up, always thundering and roaring, always getting carried away, whether he was praising or cursing you. B was also boastful, arrogant, and tyrannical; he lorded it over everyone while keeping on familiar terms with the workers, using the informal *ty* with them and always being treated as one of their own, while H, in that unique secret recipe of Russian (or russified) experts, blended both aristocracy and democracy in his manner, always using the formal *vy* with everyone and never quite fitting in with the rest of us (although he became one of us fairly quickly). Both were respected. Both were loved. The circles of B's and H's devoted fans overlapped, but did not coincide.

Here's a story: one time a military committee was on site inspecting its order of an item that, according to its specs, was supposed to be extremely durable. They'd almost passed the item when, at the very last minute, a technician accidentally dropped the thing on the floor and it split in two. It was awkward. The military committee issued a fine. So Chief Engineer H called a meeting to discuss product quality. Lots of shop heads

were present at that meeting, including B, and the lawyer Inga
Arkadyevna was there too, since fines for product quality fell
under her purview, and Pal Palych P (Pashka the fitter, aka
Pashka the champion boxer), a man both determined and
hot-tempered, and others. Everybody opined vigorously and
at length, trying to pin the blame on somebody else. Everybody interrupted everybody else. At times vicious squabbles
broke out. At some point B, without missing a beat in his tirade, stood up and loomed over the table as he barked back
at everyone left, right, and center, because it was his shop, the
finishing shop, that was the final link in the chain of production, and so of course everyone was trying to make it his fault.
Him taking that pose of his was the last straw; after that, everyone really let rip. It was such bedlam that it felt less like the
office of a defense-industry factory's chief engineer than like
a Wall Street trading floor out there in the land of the damned
capitalists. Or like the toddler room in a day care. The only
one still in her chair was Inga, all shadows and angles, who'd
recoiled from B and sat brimming with silent hostility.

H listened to the shop managers' shouting match quite
calmly, even appearing to doze off. But at one point his eyes
changed from light gray to steely. You might argue that it's not
a big difference. But everyone who was there in that office felt
it immediately. As though the light had changed, or it'd gotten colder. The bedlam started simmering down, and finally
everyone went quiet. Even B.

H raised his head and asked dryly: All done shouting?
I'm going to tell you a joke. It's a freezing-cold day. A little
bird's flying around. It freezes and falls down into the road.
A horse goes past. It poops on the little bird. The little bird
warms up and starts chirping. And a wolf comes along and
eats the little bird. The moral: if you land in a pile of shit, don't
chirp. Go do your work.

11.

Let's Go Slurp Our Camp Swill

We're on vacation. That means we're down south. That is, at the Black Sea. This is where the sea, the sun, and the south is. There's a lot of flowers and the nettles really sting. Natasha feeds her doll with rose petals and makes pretend soup out of them. An orchestra plays in the square, but with a break for the heat. It's already warm, over twenty-five degrees, at nine o'clock in the morning! Yesterday we went to the market and ate some black fish with a salted head. Today we didn't go swimming since we've already been swimming every day, and we need to take a break or else we'll get swim exhaustion. That one summer Natashka got swim exhaustion and her temperature went up to about forty degrees. I've never had such a high temperature. But one time I did fall out of a tree and break my arm. That was a few years ago. By the way, the water temperature is over twenty-four degrees. Some people live way up high, and that's really bad because they have to walk and walk to get to the water, and there's no shade there at all. But we live a little bit off to the side, where the pink buildings with the balconies are. I met Seryozhka and his brother Shurik, it turns out that they live in Leningrad on our street, there where the grocery store is on the corner. But that's actually not surprising, since their parents also work at papa's factory.

Today something interesting happened. While we were taking my bike apart a black Volga drove into our courtyard, and it was N, the Director of papa's factory. The black Volga was really dusty, and right away I could tell the Director had driven all the way from Leningrad without stopping. The whole factory that the Director runs comes here for vacation, or maybe not the whole factory, but half of it, for sure. So that's why N came out, to find out how everyone's vacations are going, but especially my father's, because they're friends. He got out of the car, the Director, and he was all red and rumpled, and he was wearing a red-and-white bucket hat, and he pulled it off his bald head, fanned himself with it, and wiped his face. Just then papa was busy taking apart my bike, but he stood right up with his dirty hands, and he and N had to shake hands some other way, not with a handshake, and so they ended up just bending in towards each other this way and that, and then papa said, welcome! The Director said, and here we have Pal Palych junior, hello, Pashka! Hello, I said. Then the Director turned to my father and said, shall we head over to the market? Oh! Let's go! said my father. I'll just wash my hands! And that's when I knew I wasn't going to get my bike that day. Unless I put it back together myself, of course. But then Director N saw I was disappointed and said, Pashka, want to wash my car? You bet your life I do! It's not every day you get this kind of luck, the chance to wash a Volga! Here, said Director N. Here's a sponge and a pail for you, and we'll just take a trip to the market in the meantime.

They went to the market, and I took the pail and ran over to the water pump where the girls were hanging around and mama was there too, sitting with Yelena Vladimirovna. Mama asked what I was so happy for, and while the pail was filling up I said that N had arrived and that I was going to wash his Volga now. Mama said, so they've gone to the market, is that it? and exchanged a look with Yelena Vladimirovna. I said, you got it! and dragged the pail back. The water inside it slopped around and splashed my feet. Then I brought over probably like ten more pails because the road from Leningrad to the south is really long and dusty. I washed the roof, and the hood, and the grill, and the headlights, and the windows, and especially the windshield, because it had mosquitoes splattered all over it. The sun was baking hotter and hotter, and even though I'd been splashing around in cold water, which didn't help by the way, I still felt like swimming and ice cream. But the good thing was that the Volga was getting prettier and prettier, I eventually got it so clean it was black and shiny all over, and everything kept burning brighter and brighter in the sun, and the ground around the car was soaked. Then I started on my bike. I thought that since I've seen other people put it together a hundred times, then I should be able to do it myself. But it turned out to be not that easy, even though I dragged the bike over into the shade and spent a long time thinking about it. ... until fifteen days later, said Director N's voice behind the bushes. Then he appeared himself, along with my father. They were walking along the path by the old dried-up apple tree and laughing. Director N was holding a string bag with bottles, and papa was holding one with apricots. Pashka! said Director N, looking at me and the Volga. That's a bang-up wash job! Thank you very much! Director N walked up to me, clapped me on the shoulder, and said: so you're probably starving, right? Well, let's go slurp our camp swill! And I thought, hmm, I didn't like the food at my camp either, but I'm not sure I know that word swill.

We went to eat lunch. We called mama and Natasha, and for lunch we had the usual: cold borscht, potatoes, and tomatoes and cucumbers, and then tea. The grown-ups also had wine. There wasn't any camp swill, as far as I could tell. After all, borscht isn't swill, and neither are apricots. We sat outside, as usual, at a big table. Director N smoked and cracked a ton of jokes, especially with Natasha, who still doesn't understand jokes, and so it's super funny to joke around with her, and I waited for a good time and then asked papa surreptitiously: but where's the swill? What swill? my father whispered back. The swill that Director N said we'd have, he said "let's go slurp our camp swill." Shhh, said my father, and that's all he said. Pashka, the director asked my father, what's the little guy asking about? He's asking what camp swill is. Director N gave a short laugh.

And then we managed to break mama's resistance and so we all went swimming after all. The hottest part of the day had just ended and there were lots and lots of people! Mama always hates that, but we love it. The more people there are, the more fun it is, how does she not understand that! But mama hates it because she's afraid we might get lost without her noticing, or drown without her noticing. At the seashore in the south, everybody strips down to their underwear, and you can really see which of the men were in the war. From a distance you can see that lots of them still have all their arms and legs, but when you go down to the water and look at all their backs and bodies, you're just amazed how some of them managed to stay alive after such wounds. The one good thing is that we socked it to the Fritzes a whole lot worse. That'll teach them. And I've already tried floating on my back a little bit, and I've gone into the water twelve times.

That evening we played Cossacks and robbers and we played so hard we didn't notice when it got completely dark. In the dark Seryozhka plopped right down on a nettle and yelled something awful. And there's also these red berries growing behind our building, I don't know what they're called. They taste like a mix of spruce tree and pencil lead. And then mama called us in for supper and bedtime, and while I was washing my hands I remembered that word and I asked mama, what's camp swill? Is it good? Mama was washing dishes. She answered, no. But what's it made of, anyway? Have you tasted it? Swill is any yucky, watery soup, and it doesn't matter what it's made of. You make it out of whatever you *have* to make it out of. Rotten potatoes, for example. I went to bed. I dreamed of the orchestra's red music, and of the bright sunny water in the bucket, and how it drips off the sparkling black Volga, and how the bright, golden chains of sunlight glitter in the sea.

12.

The Aster

Today the ocean is tinged pink, multicolored, and the sun above it is greenish, and the air trembles from the heat as it does over an enormous field of buckwheat. Today the ocean breathes evenly and deeply, first lifting, then lowering our trade vessel. We're with the Black Sea Maritime Shipping Fleet. We're headed to Cuba and we're bringing our Aster with us: the first Soviet radar system for the merchant fleet, developed right in our very own Freedom Factory, now to be installed on all large ships without exception. I'm standing next to our Aster, with the open ocean around me on all sides; there's neither shores nor ships to be seen, just the immense breadth, calm, and expanse of the sea. We're headed to Cuba, and the ocean is with us, and our Aster is with us, and forty officers are with us, and I'm teaching them to use her. All the officers really like the Aster. It was as though she'd been created specifically for difficult navigational situations, for example, like when it's six or seven on the Douglas scale and you need to bring your ship out of port by maneuvering around the other vessels while remaining inside the narrow navigational channel.

Today the ocean is tinged pink, like a field of buckwheat in bloom, like in my childhood, when I didn't know anything about any ocean yet, I only knew fields, where it was tractors, not ships, that went cruising around and owned the place. The ocean is tinged pink, and glows, and it's deserted all the way to the horizon, but the round screen of my Aster shows that there is actually someone there. There didn't used to be any radars like the Aster before, and back when I was a midshipman going on my first circumnavigation, I had a pretty rough time of it.

We're headed for Cuba, we're getting closer to Cuba, we're a peaceful trade vessel, and this time that's really true: we're not covering up any submarines, nobody's hiding in our shadow. But the Americans aren't napping. First the round screen of my Aster shows it, then I see it myself: he's coming. He's coming in on a low, skimming trajectory, and I really want to say "Hi!" to him somehow, but I can't think how. And then I know exactly how.

There's never been a radar like our Aster before. And there aren't any others like our Aster now, either. Because our Aster is dual-band. There's an X-band, a 3.5-centimeter wave band that's traditional for big trade vessels, and an S-band, a 10-centimeter wave band that's stronger and can go farther. Submarines typically use it. The ocean is tinged pink, glistening; the sun is high; and a Yankee is flying around our ship, not finding anything suspicious, so he flies on, and I switch the Aster from the X-band to the other band. The S-band.

Our head design engineer, W, who designed the Aster, is also here on the ship with us. And it's worth telling a tale or two about him! Our Aster's head design engineer is a real seafarer, a real sea wolf! During the war he was second-in-command on the Liberty ships, you know, those ships that brought in food and weapons on the Lend-Lease program, the Germans used to sink them by the hundreds, it was like a sport for them, sinking Liberty ships, and anyway it was incredibly risky, and when the war ended they kicked W out of the army for hitting the sauce, and then he quit drinking cold turkey but he didn't go back to the army, he went and got an engineering degree, he was already over thirty, even back then, and now he's fifty, but even with that age difference he and I are really good friends, and that's why I'm the one he took abroad with him, nobody else from Freedom is allowed to go abroad, 'cause we're a secret factory, after all, but our Aster isn't secret, she's for civil use, so have at it, Yankee, get a good look at her, look and listen all you want! Seems like you're a few cards shy of a full deck, Yankee, you're circling our ship for the sixth time and I can read your mind (with Aster's help): but there's got to be a submarine there... but there's not!... but there is!... but there's not!...

And then I switch back to the X-band again.

Our W always wears a captain's cap. He smokes cigars he stocks up on in port. He also writes books: historical ones, scientific, technical, all kinds. Our W can do anything. Once when we were in port in Germany, there was a storm, and nobody could bring the ship out to sea in that kind of weather. And then the captain of one German ship comes on board to us and says, we heard that the designer of the Aster radar's on your vessel, is that right? That's right, we say. So then they started in on him, begging and pleading with our W to bring the ship out to sea himself. At first W wouldn't go along with it, but finally he went ahead and brought the ship on out, and it was the only ship that got out to sea that day...

Right when the Yankee had calmed down and was about to fly away, I switch over again. The S-band! Back he comes! This time so low that I can see him. And he can see us. Every little detail. He can see the fish that's lying around everywhere on our deck under the golden sun—we catch it, hang it up to dry, and then smoke it down in the hold. He can see me, in my shirt and sandals, and he can see the Aster. So I point to our radar for him, and laugh and wave. The Yankee gets boiling mad. On the next pass he shakes his fist at me, enraged, and he's guffawing! And I laugh and I shake my fist too! We're guffawing and threatening each other! Yeah, he'd figured it out, he'd figured out what was going on, damned if he didn't! So there we are, guffawing and threatening each other, and the ocean shines under us, pink as a buckwheat field in flower, and the sky glows.

13.

Four Mimosas by November 7th

I'm a berserker on the job. Even now I'm not all that easy to get along with; what must it've been like back then, when I was young and had the fire in my belly!

So we're doing the Mimosa. That's twelve whole cabinets like this, plus wheels and cables. That's sixteen rockets firing underwater and going seven thousand kilometers, each one taking out four targets. A big deal back then.

Those days I was an assembly fitter, lead man in my shop bay. I hadn't yet embarked, as people usually put it, on my career. I just came to the factory and did my job. I didn't know anything about any careers back then.

It took me a while to figure out how to do everything. At first, I couldn't do anything right. I thought, to hell with it all, I'm quitting… I was even going to run off and be a technician in the Antarctic. But Director N talked me out of it. I wouldn't say he cussed me out exactly, but the look on his face was all it took. That's when I started wanting to turn my life around.

So I stayed at Freedom. Gradually, step by step, I started getting promoted. Every four years I got a new title. Senior fitter, then lead man of my shop bay.

We're doing the Mimosa. From the beginning of April to the end of September we finish three. All the shops are working three shifts. Nobody's taking any vacation.

The end of September rolls around. That's when B, the head of my shop, calls me in... He was a legendary guy. Just like me. Lively, impressionable, explosive.

B calls me in and says, you know, F, here's the thing, four more Mimosas have to be ready by November 7th. I say, if that's what you need, that's what we'll do.

I didn't know anything. What the big rush was all about, why they needed it by the anniversary of the October Revolution. All I know is my nuts and bolts.

So we got to it. The main thing is to talk with everybody and convince them to work. I convinced everybody. Everybody agreed. Off we went and busted our guts. Two days we worked round the clock, three days. On the fourth night, finally, we went back home. Then back to work the next morning.

After eight days of working like that, B comes in and takes a look around, sees how much we've done. He takes a look and sees it's not enough. But you said you'd do it. So I come back at him: we will do it. Now our B, he always knew who was capable of what, and he made no bones about saying so. I saw that he'd begun to doubt me. It got me worried, of course.

After work, there I am, running to the metro station again so I don't miss the last train. I barely made it. Back then I lived out on Education Prospect, the metro didn't get out that far, I had to take the trolleybus from Finland Station to the end of the line and then walk.

I'm the last passenger on the trolleybus, we're halfway there, and the trolleybus stops next to Piskaryov Cemetery. That's it, says the driver, get out, I can turn around here. I'm not going all the way out to the end turnaround. I say, you can't do this. He says, you can't do anything about it.

It's one fifteen in the morning. I have to be back at the factory tomorrow. I've still got to walk about seven kilometers to get home. It's October, weather's cold and windy, mixed rain and snow. But what else can I do? I head through the cemetery for home.

I'm walking along and all of a sudden I feel that I just can't go on. I'm dead on my feet. I'm done. Good thing there was a bench right there. I was wearing this kind of canvas jacket. I lay down, pulled my hood over my eyes, and I was out. It didn't even occur to me that I might freeze. I just lay down and was out like a light.

And then I had an astonishing dream. I've never had dreams like that since.

I dreamed that I was swimming in the depths of the ocean. Around me, at the corners of what would be a kind of gigantic square, there are four submarines. They look like matryoshkas. Two are ours, and two are American. They're suspended in the depths of the water and are waiting for something. And I'm swimming in the middle of that square. I've got to drink, I need to. But I can't open my mouth. And there's nothing in the ocean that can slake my thirst.

But I seem to be able to breathe okay.

Those four matryoshkas are all different. One's big, and kind of fat, stocky. Another one's tall and quite slim. The third is just plain small. The fourth is average. And one of them also had this thing kind of like a diadem with searchlights on its head, and the diadem was rotating and sending signals with the lights.

And these matryoshkas were talking with each other in the air, over the radio waves. I'm in the depths of the ocean and I can hear them. And suddenly I start to realize that they're talking about me. "This thoughtless comrade," they say, "who's he for?" Meaning they thought I had to take a side. Either ours or America's. And quick. I had to make some kind of decision. Or else this very moment, because of me, the Third World War will break out. And it'll all be my fault.

But it's really hard for me to make a decision, see. I have water under my arms and legs, like layers of, I don't know, like layers of plastic. The water bends around me, and my mouth is dry as dust, I have this terrible urge to open my mouth and drink my fill of water, but I can't, I'm not allowed.

Then I gather the last of my strength and start pushing the water with my arms and legs, just slamming it. Suddenly, I fall deeper. I've heard that this does happen in the depths of the ocean: there's heavy water and light water, different layers. I'd fallen into some heavy water and dropped like a stone right onto the seabed. The matryoshkas were still up above. It was getting darker and darker around me. And I had this terrible desire to drink. For some reason I was getting hotter and hotter, and I could tell that I was on fire. And I realized that this is it, this is our Earth melting down, because I hadn't managed to take a side and so the Third World War had started, the rockets and bombs had started flying.

That was when I woke up. I jump off the bench, gasping for air. What'd happened is that while I was sleeping, the snow'd started falling faster and covered me up. If I hadn't woken up, I'd've turned into a popsicle. I'd slept all of two hours. But I wasn't sleepy.

I went back to the street. I waited an hour for the trolleybus. And I went back to the factory and my workshop.

This is the strange thing: after that I didn't get sleepy at all. The whole month of October. I didn't even bother going home. I'd just call my wife sometimes, check in on things. I slept every third night, and even then for just two or three hours. But I wasn't sleepy. I'd doze an hour or two in the shop, and then I was good as new. That was just the level of enthusiasm I had for the work, that's all.

So I worked and worked and by the seventh of November I'd put together four Mimosas. Four! That's an insane amount of work! I don't know how I did it!

Half a year later, in May, the head of our shop, B, was celebrating his fiftieth birthday in the Moscow Hotel on Uprising Square. Director N'd been invited. B and his wife Shura are sitting at the head of the table, and there's N and his wife.

We'd all been assigned toasts. I'm somewhere down around number thirty on the list. Not a figure with close ties to the emperor. And it took so long to get to me, that... No matter how hard you try to drink just a little bit, it's still the thirtieth toast, you get my drift...

So basically, I went up there onto the platform with them, I said something, I don't even remember what, and I left. People told me about it later. Director N elbows our shop head, B, and asks, who the heck was that, anyway?

And what people say is that B answered, who, that? That's F, the one who put together four Mimosas in thirty days.

These are the kind of things that put hair on your chest!

14.
Ball Bearings

The main thing in life is to know how to make it beautiful, you know. After all, there's no such thing as work you love. Not until you learn to fall in love with it. When I was little, I didn't like washing the floor. So I always made things up. We had this painted floor, you know, this royal blue paint that was all peeling. When you'd just washed it, and it was wet, it was so bright it glowed. And the parts where the paint had peeled looked like clouds or something. And you could imagine they were cloud-wreathed mountains and valleys. You'd be washing the floor and imagining you were wiping the dirt off the sky. That's the kind of work you don't get every day, wiping off the sky! And I'd get so involved in it that sometimes I'd be surprised afterward to see that it was cloudy outside: how can that be? I just wiped off the whole sky!

People also say that back then, back when we were young, everyone was the same, they tried to make everyone the same. But the people who say that are the people who want to slough all the responsibility for their own lives off on someone else. Take me, for example. (I really like taking myself as an example, so you'll just have to bear with me.) Back when I was a schoolgirl we all wore uniforms. The whole time, even senior year. A black pinafore, black or brown bows, and white collars and cuffs. I always took pains to make my cuffs different, not like everyone else's. I found a pattern and made myself a little set of collar and cuffs, you do this tiny cutwork in linen and then finish all the cut edges with a satin stitch in white thread, it's called Richelieu embroidery! And I was even willing to iron every inch of it, every day! Then I learned to sew really well and all my life I sewed outfits for myself. You know what I sewed my wedding dress out of? Parachute silk! Back then K and I lived next to the aerodrome, where all those, you know, where they all used to train, and there was lots of that parachute silk, with just the most amazing green sheen. I just about killed myself sewing that dress! You know where that was? That was down there by Mozhayskiy, down where Taytsy is, all that stuff... The headquarters for the air defense forces for the entire northwest region was there, it covered from Murmansk all the way to Kaliningrad. K supplied it with equipment from our factory, but me, I had to go back into the city to the factory every day, an hour and a half there and an hour and a half back. We had a little house there, now it'd just be a dacha, but back then we lived there, had our little stove there, we didn't even know what these communal apartments were all about! Can you imagine? We had our own little hacienda, we were perfectly independent, and that back in Soviet times! I don't understand all that digging around in each other's domestic dirt, where everybody knows how many times everybody else went to the bathroom... Sure, we had to light the stove and keep it going, we had to get the little tyke to school and back every day, and there were all the lines, too, we just didn't have a thing... so sure, in some ways it was very hard, you look back on it now and just cringe. But you know what? The thing is that you can portray any life as an unhappy one. You know how you could tell the story of my life, if you put a little effort into it? I'd end up crying my eyes out, and so would you. But what's the point of that, I ask you? Why get melodramatic, why emphasize the negative, when you can cheerfully emphasize the positive, let go of the negative, and live a happy life? Look at me, even now... See, they tell me—the doctors, they're pretty straightforward these days—they tell it like it is, a six percent chance, life expectancy two and a half years. They don't beat around the bush, not one bit. We've got a whole cemetery full of people like you, they say. And I get what they're saying, I do... but I just can't bring myself to think about death. Sometimes I even sit and try to do it, on purpose, but it doesn't work. All I see is some kind of yellow blob. That's it. So obviously it's just not something that is necessary for me to see. The bottom line is that I get it, I am aware that you've got to pay the piper. But my life was very happy, I loved my work.

I really loved my work. The Boss, now he was something, he worked our tails off! I mean A. Everybody in the EDB, that's the Experimental Design Bureau to you, called him the Boss. And it was interesting, too, we had fun at work. So then you come home and start cooking the soup, but your head is still full of adjustments and improvements. When you go to bed, you put a notebook and pen under your pillow. You wake up in the night with some idea in your head so you grab your notebook, write it down, and go back to a sound sleep. The next day when you get in, you describe the idea to the rest of the team, and find that there really is something to it. So everyone discusses it, and then everyone gets down to work.

It's actually very difficult to say what a person's individual contribution to the work is, when you work collectively. Once in a while it really does turn out that the idea pretty much came to you alone; but would you've had the idea if you hadn't been surrounded by these exact people? One person tosses out one little word, the next one adds on to it, expands it, and then the third one writes it all down... and then yet another person formulates it clearly... and so which of them was it, I ask you? Hmm? Which one? And that's why I believe in collective work. I don't believe that when you sit all by yourself you can—everything comes out of discussion, or after the discussion. It all basically comes out of that environment. And our EDB, it was just that kind of conducive environment... It was alive, like primordial soup. Like dough. The atmosphere at the factory and in our bureau was very good. You see, it was... canned, if you will, preserved back when they hadn't started lying yet. Now I remember that transition, when all the lying started, quite clearly. When I was little, back when I was in school, there weren't any lies yet. That is, maybe there were some, but not down at our level, not down where we were. They were out there, separate, above us, and they hadn't soaked down through to us, they hadn't insinuated themselves into the fabric of simple, everyday life. And want to know why that was? I think it was because of the enormous potential after the war. The country had won the war, and that by itself was so much happiness, so much truth, that it lasted for the next couple of decades. And it really was a genuinely happy time. Everyone worked sincerely, taught and learned sincerely, and believed in happiness, and it had nothing to do with communism, not a whit; it was a kind of... it was breadth, expansion... and then we put a man in space. We lived in space, all of us! Even if there were six of us to a room in the dorm, we all still lived in space. In the Universe! There was no iron curtain! Space is the absence of chaos, it's clarity and order, and at the same time it's infinity... and there we were, inhabiting this infinity... Well, then in the seventies, of course, that's when the lies began, it was all clearly visible and obvious; but not at our factory! Not in our EDB! We still had this kind of little island where there were absolutely no lies. I don't know how that happened. Maybe it was because of the people. It was definitely the people.

And we also had such fun. Such fun we had. We were always having some kind of little celebration. It was our second home. We celebrated everyone's birthdays. I used to make wine at home, whole big batches of it. You know what I used? Currants and gooseberries. Alcohol was banned from the factory, you couldn't just bring it in through the front gate, but if you pour the wine into a three-liter jar it looks just like juice, and there you go. You walk into the bureau and it's come on, folks, have some juice! Is it *that* juice? Oh, it's *that* juice all right. And once when there wasn't anything else to do, we... basically the factory was making ball bearings for bicycles, and one lot ended up defective. I'd made myself a dress, so I decorated it, sewed on those defective bearings. And you can just imagine, there I go, walking down the street, and every man in sight is turning around staring at me! At first I was flattered, but later I realized: those bearings were deficit goods, right? And there go these men, each thinking the exact same thing: where did that little idiot get them all?!

15.

Off-Camera

The camera is preserving a historical moment: the signing of the memorandum transferring the Freedom Factory to a new director. It's a sunny day outside. The small office is packed with people. A side table and two armchairs stand on an improvised stage. Director N's in the armchair on the left. He settles down in the seat, gets comfortable, takes up a pen, bends over the paper and writes his signature for the last time. That's it! From now on, the former factory director will be an honored pensioner. What should he expect now? Money? Yes. Travel? A little. A car and a free trip to a health resort? As much as his heart desires.

Director N smiles. In the first row sits B, the head of Shop Nineteen, potbelly front and center. B thinks, "I'm fucked."

Next to B, the head of Shop Nineteen, sits the head of the tool-making shop. He thinks, "Right here next to me sits B. That's who should've been made director. B is a larger-than-life figure, while this V looks like pretty small beer. Wonder how many kilos he even weighs anyway. If you put N on one side of a teeter-totter and say five Vs on the other side, N would still outweigh them all."

The ranks are arrayed, silent and solid. And in this silence, it feels like something just has to happen, right there in front of everybody. And it does happen. Just not in front of everybody. It's hard to even imagine that N is going to stop being director, that somebody completely different will run the factory now. It's simply impossible to imagine. And even though N himself chose V to be his successor, even though V has already been the director of an enormous factory for many years, one he'd built himself, along with residential districts for the workers and a wastewater treatment plant—even so, it's impossible to imagine. Engineer H, who worked with N his whole life, thinks, "But how will we..." and proceeds to think about all those intensely secret ideas that N had shared with him alone. How will we do that now? Am I really going to have to share them with V? That's impossible. I will never get used to it, H thinks; and gradually, still thinking this, gets used to it.

Meanwhile V speaks his seven ringing phrases, takes up a pen and hastily places his signature. It's sloppy and slants upward. Applause. Now V is director. The head of the galvanizing shop sneers and thinks, a real-life Tom Thumb. We'll show him. He doesn't have the slightest idea where he's landed. Intellectual. B thinks, "I'm going to be sick." What this means is: I'm going to be sick.

But at some point it had to happen, because... well, it's just more than one person can physically do, working so much; after all, look at what a life he'd had. The war, the blockade... In the war N was young, still under thirty, but he was already director of a factory that made radio equipment for partisans. Back under Stalin. Then a prison term. Then he brought Freedom up by its bootstraps. At some point, you know, it just starts taking its toll on your health.

So then he and H, who was chief engineer at the time, quietly approached V and started trying to convince him to take the reins of command. Now despite his scatterbrained demeanor, V is also a person of consequence. For many years he was the director of an enormous factory, he had built an entire brand-new enterprise from the ground up in Vyatka, and it wasn't just the factory itself, he'd also built entire residential districts for the workers *and* a wastewater treatment plant. There he sits in his armchair, facing N, and nobody has the faintest idea what he's going to do first and what's going to wait until later. But V, he's going to do some unexpected things. For example, let's take... there's one very characteristic story about merging the workshops. V is going to merge Shops Seventeen and Nineteen again. Back when N separated them, it was just a technical issue: the kind of work the finishing shop did required more training. But V is merging them again. And why is that? Why, it's to put an end to the constant arguments, infighting, and internecine warfare: "us in the fitting shop, we do all the work, but those finishers get all the credit; they're white-collar workers, but we take the rap for them." And so V merges these shops again because the human factor has grown important, as has the element of good governance, good management, and now a single unbroken chain of command is required, where everything isn't just taken for granted and business as usual, where everything is clearly defined, it's clear who's responsible for what, so there's no stepping on toes and fobbing things off on others. Would that kind of consideration ever occur to N? Perhaps. To B? Psshh! That's what I'm saying.

Everyone's clapping. Now that thin one there's stepped up and is saying something with a smile, that's T, the head design engineer on a series of instruments from the EDB. Here's the audience again. The expressions on people's faces are complicated. Why not B? Well, we already explained why not B, although god knows, we could always be wrong. Lots of people don't like that the times are changing, but there's no getting around it. Under N, the arms race was moving along full speed, and people didn't think about it at all, they didn't even conceptualize things along those lines. But when the arms race subsided, then it hit them that they had to change their style of leadership now, and figure out how to get their manufacturing and production on track, because now the worker wasn't just a detail, a spare part, but a person, and now he needed a different motivation to work, you needed different kinds of carrots for different people, and basically it was time for everyone to tear their eyes away from their machines and look around and see what the heck was going on... And N understands that V, with his openness, flexibility, and liveliness, even with that little whiff of risky dealings—V is more suited to the role of being that kind of leader...

N polishes his glasses. He has collapsed heavily back into his armchair. There's some kind of lingering discomfort, or awkwardness, or maybe it just looks that way from the outside, maybe it's we viewers who are reading it into the situation. It looks as though N still hasn't fully grasped what just happened. He had to steel himself for this, too, of course. For giving away the factory that he basically built. So yes, we don't really know, maybe it wasn't all as lovey-dovey as it looks here.

And there they go, exchanging ceremonial kisses on the cheek just as friendly as you please. You can't act any other way with V, though. He takes a look at you, then he mirrors you, reflects you, charms you. Feels as though once he's alone with himself, V must stop existing, since he's no longer necessary. Many people won't ever come to like him because of that. It'll look to them like the pretense comprising V's basic core is incompatible with sincerity and depth. After all, N knew many of our workers by name, and he'd always be scouring the shops. It goes without saying that V won't know any of the workers by name; heck, he'll direct things pretty much without ever coming out of his office...

Look at that, look, everybody's clapping, but this one guy's sitting there and he's not clapping, see, he's propped on his elbows, he's watching with complete attention: what on earth are we doing, citizens, where are we headed, who is this we're just giving our factory to, he's a bit too spry, this comrade, if he goes and perches on our N's chair his feet won't even reach the ground.

But V will reach new heights.

So that's the ceremonial kissing. It requires V to stretch up, while N has to bend over with some difficulty. And now they're going to shake hands for a long, long time, and you can tell that V's grip isn't as strong as N's, he can't shake hands that long, and so V begins beaming, a smile just bursts out onto his face, and when the people in the audience see that smile, the expressions on their faces change, going from complicated to more complicated, and certain people shift in their seats, while the one who wasn't clapping leans forward with his whole entire body, still propped on his elbows, and he's holding his chin in one big broad mitt so it covers up his mouth, all we can see are his dark, glittering eyes. And that's the last frame.

16.

Sea Trials

On the wall hangs a cross-stitched rug—rather, a rug embroidered with little crosses—that is, with little x's. Kilometers of water and a deep floor are down below, and up above are gray skies and little hillocks. Here's a yellow x walking through the hillocks. It's comrade D from Odessa in the insulated coat his wife sewed him; he breathes fire as he goes, in his yellow coat with purple pockets. He goes along the path winding between the hillocks, and unfamiliar critters peer out at him from behind them. An immensely strong wind's blowing, and has been for more than two weeks, so that now, of all the snow that had been on the hillocks, only the path is left. The path is well tamped, and the snow sticks better on it. In winter, when the wind swept up big drifts, that path looked like a trench between steep dunes, but now the dunes have melted and the wind's worn them away, and the path's turned into the Great Wall of China, a bridge, and there goes D, balancing on this slippery bridge, bent double in his yellow coat that catches the wind like a sail. D breathes fire made of sunny, garlicky soup, and vodka, and aspirin, and coughs like he's at death's door. Nothing you can do about it. (We pull back, and see it again: gray on gray, with the little bone of the submarine inside.)

Sea trials for the submarine and all the instruments on it take twelve days. They do a deep-water dive, three hundred meters. Engineers and military reps packed tight as sardines. Everyone sitting on benches in a stuffy, cramped space. Lots of food, wan lighting. They sit in utter silence, listening for leaks. The sub is under pressure, after all, and if there's a leak anywhere, they'll hear it. Everyone's sitting there and every single one of them, depending on the vigor of his imagination, pictures an oceanic hammer/vice/fist, squeezing the sub like an egg/shell/cucumber. Only a few of them have complete faith, trusting utterly in their fate. Our D's one of these. He's serene, almost cheerful, even, but it's not that abnormal cheeriness that usually means someone's manic from staying awake all night; it's more that naturally round, calm kind of cheer. And he's coughing, of course. This is what happens before the sea trials (we zoom in again): everyone has to pair up and get into an icy-cold pool of rusty, cloudy water. In diving suits, naturally. They let you down to around four meters, you walk around on a tether for a while, and then they pull you back out. Still with us? Still here. Once D got tangled up with G, an engineer from a big manufacturer of submarine communications systems. The water was cloudy, of course, couldn't see a thing, and these two big-time engineers are down there feeling their way around. They walked in circles for a while and got completely tangled up. Getting them out was a royal pain.

Five klicks into the hillocks: the path winds through hillocks, skies are gray, and the ocean's right there. D has a coughing fit. Ugh, I'm sweating like a pig! D, big and round, extracts a canteen from the depths of his down jacket. It's five kilometers from home to the pier. The romance of it. Two hundred men on one boat, every single instrument serviced by its own team of engineers and finishing technicians. D the Odes-

is paired up with Vitya P, the famous millionaire of the northern latitudes. Everybody knows you can bring in good money during sea trials, but the persistent Vitya has made it into a principle. He's determined to show that a regular Soviet laborer doing honest work really can make enough to buy three two-bedroom apartments in Leningrad. Of course, D's not just twiddling his thumbs, either. Recently he found himself in one of those completely ordinary, everyday situations: he and his wife and kid were going to go to Leningrad (he had to get recertified every six months), and they were going to stay for a week, as usual. Do some shopping, see some shows, get together with the family, that kind of thing. As soon as they arrive at the airport, Ninochka goes, "Mama, I'm going to be sick." His wife goes, "We'll be back in a minute," and disappears with Ninka. What the hell! D goes running all over the waiting area, they've given the boarding announcement, but no sign of wife or child! D runs to the administrator, to the airport police... their names are announced over the loudspeaker... not a trace of them. He races over, but boarding is over, and they're nowhere to be found. Turned out they'd gone back home. They'd just decided not to go on the trip. It happens. But the thing is that the plane that they'd almost flown off in crashed with no survivors. Both his wife and D quickly forgot about this incident, and of course it had nothing to do with the fact that six months later they would move back to Leningrad. It was just that she was pregnant again, and Ninochka was starting school.

The terminal appears in the distance. D the Odessan feels better already. He made it! He didn't blow away in the wind! Tomorrow they will head out, so right now the vessel is crawling with people, all tinkering with this, re-soldering that. Business as usual (gloats D). Some ships don't make it out for days, but not us: we're ready to go. Vitka P tugs on D's sleeve: pssst, D! Nothing's working. What do you mean? Why not? I mean nothing even turns on... D breaks into a sweat. He scratches his curly head and unbuttons his yellow coat. The remains of the garlicky soup have evaporated. Hold on a minute, I'll open it up.

He opens it up. He looks inside. He parts the device's guts and shines a flashlight into them. He looks, but doesn't find anything. Because sometimes you can get every tech in the finishing shop to look, and still not figure it out. D is mad as hell. It's past seven, and it's getting dark. They're heading out tomorrow. Vitka paces in circles. They look at it together. Fuck! I got it! D yells. The lid's warped! Agh, those morons! How'd they paint this lid?! It's just like they say: no such thing as a minor detail in this line of work. Shave down the paint, maybe? No, then the seal won't be hermetic. What do we do? That's when D finds a little metal washer, wraps it in three layers of electrical tape, and sticks it under the lid, so the contacts meet when it closes. And now we turn it on... (Drumroll.) We have contact! D releases all his pent-up coughing in one deafening paroxysm. Vitka looks around. If the military reps find out about this, they could sue us. We did submit the prototype without a washer wrapped in electrical tape, after all! But who's gonna go in there besides us? Even if it does break down, we'll be the ones who open it up to fix it. The lid is screwed down tight. It works! It works! Vitka P and D the Odessan's moods lift dramatically. They cast a (victorious) glance at the others.

An enormous rug on the wall, a cross-stitched wool rug. Gray waves meet and merge over the little bone of the submarine. Two hundred people inside, military reps and engineers, keeping quiet as the grave. Silence and a measured, ominous humming. D tries not to cough. He's thinking about the washer. Never mind. To hell with the washer. Relax. So, are we going to launch? It was about two years ago now when the missiles went the wrong way. They were headed for friendly China, you see. If they'd gotten there, it wouldn't've been pretty. Luckily, we managed to knock them down. The engineers sit, each thinking about his washer, or his copper wire, or something else along those lines. They think for a long time. The launch window is closing, but nothing's happening. An officer comes in. His face expresses placid desperation. Everyone tries to figure out what's going on. So, are we? Launching them? No, we're not. We're not going to launch them today. Stand down, comrades. Some hunters went out into the taiga in sector seventeen. Hunters!? Of all the fucking…!! They had to pick now! Couldn't somebody have warned them!? We're going home. The next attempt will be in three weeks.

D the Odessan is the first to break down laughing. Then other people start laughing too. Washers! moans D, forgetting it's top secret. Electrical tape! Hunters! Ha-ha-ha!

17.

May Day

And here's our May Day parade. (The Land of the Soviets joyfully celebrates the First of May. Red banners, gigantic signs, cheerful songs and the sound of orchestras, an endless sea of participants in this mass demonstration.) White sky above, asphalt below, the Kirov department store building is visible in the background. The Freedom Factory workers always brought up the rear, behind the marchers from the Putilov Factory (the Kirov Factory). That exact moment is what's on the screen right now: a huge group of us standing there in the wind, waiting. It's clear and windy out, looks like it was very cold that day. F, thirty-two years old, is standing over to the left, on the borderline separating the seen from the unseen. He's thirty-two. And because the camera's filming not him, but the women standing next to him—because the camera is on them, and he has fallen into the frame without knowing it—F is gazing pensively over toward the Narva Gate, where he'd seen hanged Germans as a child, during the Blockade.

(The Soviet people have begun an extremely critical stage of the Five-Year Plan. In essence, this year will determine the outcome of the Plan for the entire country. The Central Statistical Administration of the USSR has announced our achievements in fulfilling the Plan, indicating our industry's sure strides forward, our grand new successes.)

Here we have two women in overcoats, chatting. The hems of their light-colored coats flare out in the May wind. They're wearing spike-heeled pumps. They each hold a carnation. The one on the left, the pretty one, with full lips on a thin face, wipes away a tear and smiles. The tear is also because of the wind. A factory family flashes momentarily onscreen: a strapping little girl in a fuzzy knit hat waves a small red flag, and another laughing tyke holding a balloon sits on his papa's shoulders. What the film can convey: sun, wind, balloons, the high sky, flags large and small, a banner on a truck ("Glory to the Communist Party of the Soviet Union"), rows of hammer-and-sickles along the sides of the truck, and on its back, bright letters in relief spell FREEDOM (the name of the factory looks like a slogan). What the film can't convey: the smells of a Leningrad factory on a cold, sunny day, the smells of a fresh sea wind, asphalt, and iron filings, the smells of brick, bitumen, concrete, creosote, new grass, earth, machine oil, smoke.

(Veterans who fought in the Great Fatherland War march in festive formation accompanied by the working class's younger generation, which is continuing the efforts of its fathers and mothers. Among these young people are shock-workers of communist labor and leading industrial workers. It is the patriotic duty of every Soviet man and woman to mark this holiday with new achievements on the labor front.)

Here comes our factory's top brass. That strapping fellow striding briskly along in the long overcoat and hat is the second director of Freedom, the legendary N himself. To the right of N is B, the loud, unruly head of assembly operations, an exceptional worker and inveterate binge drinker. Time and again the issue of dealing with him was put on the agenda, but time and again it was taken back off: how could we even have a factory without B? Instead he would always write repentant explanatory statements about moral character. After

N retired, everyone thought that B would be named director, but he wasn't, of course. To the left of N is O, our production planner and economist. Back then he was still the factory's new kid on the block. All three of them are deep in animated conversation. They're all in a good mood. B is laughing, N is talking and gesticulating, and O, smiling, waves at the camera with a red carnation. Behind them are the best lady skier in the factory, and our coquette fatale, and fashionable, mustachioed youths in dark glasses, and I, "the longest legs in the EDB," and a captivated little Young Pioneer with his ratty jacket all unbuttoned, and the guffawing head of the repair shop, a jack of all trades and an utter charmer, gloved hands holding a child-sized flag on a thin wooden dowel rod, and the Little Octobrist twins, cute as buttons with their gap teeth, and the passionate, but no longer young accountant, and a bevy of painter ladies from Shop Thirteen, and the young Miss Z, the galvanic coatings specialist, and U, the ascetic head designer of the strategically important device 5T-42R. The camera jiggles. All the buildings (this is along Old Peterhof Prospect, used to be Gas Prospect) are bathed in blinding sunlight. The windows glitter like ultraviolet stars.

(Children, a great many children, are lifted high above the heads of marchers in the victorious columns. Children are our hope, they are our present and our future. The workers of our factory continue the glorious traditions of the heroic working class of the Narva Outpost, bringing to life Lenin's precept: "We will achieve the victory of communist labor.")

What the film can't convey: one time a delegation of communists from one of the rebellious Latin American republics turned up at Freedom, and they asked the Komsomol members: "The revolutionary movement was born in your country. So tell us, how? What methods did you use to organize your underground, to coordinate a real revolution?" The Komsomol

members grew sad. But this is what the film can convey: here comes a military orchestra, instruments flashing in the bright sunlight, a bugler playing with one hand and holding a home-made music stand in the other. The last person on the left, the trombone player, is glancing over at the sheet music. The bugler, on the right, in the cap, is a colorful character of about fifty, with a strong build and muttonchops, wearing his coat wide open. Behind them: a woman wearing a fuzzy knitted hat and holding a balloon, three workers arm-in-arm, dark faces, hats, smiles, "The Party and the People Are One," "Glory to the Leaders of Industry," a little girl in a checkered coat and a kerchief, an elderly couple in identical dark overcoats, the tops of the trees above Volynkina Street. Oh, yes, and the brass cymbals!

(In the columns of demonstrators from the city's Kirov district march workers from our factory. Alongside their mentors, veterans of labor, march young workers who are honored with continuing to keep watch over the Five-Year Plan and exemplifying a conscientious approach to each of their entrusted tasks, completing their duties in a timely fashion while maintaining the highest quality.)

Somehow, though, this scene just leaves me feeling depressed, I don't know why. There I am, marching in the crowd, happily waving around my portrait of Suslov. I'd insistently volunteered to carry a portrait, any portrait; we got ten rubles for it. I'm walking along gabbing with a plump, attractive lady who's belly-laughing, her permed hair escaping from under her kerchief, I don't remember what color it was, but she's wearing dark lipstick and in the film's bright sunlight her lips are overexposed, black. Her name was Raisa. She was the best dispatcher in the factory, she was pretty much made for the job. But then her husband's brother married a foreigner and left, moved to Israel, and so within twenty-four hours Raisa was transferred from the dispatch office to somewhere in accounting. A few years ago I found out that she and her whole family have been living in America for a long time now. But why on earth does it cause such pangs of grief... after all, the grief isn't welling up because it's a Communist demonstration and not a voluntary popular holiday, because the people at it basically aren't free people. It's not because of that. But the grief also isn't because we were young back then, and now we're old men. No. It's the film's own inherent grief, an aesthetic grief, and I think it's actually the sun that's intensifying it, because I know, after all, that regardless of the sun it's a cold May out there on those festive streets, and everyone's hands are getting frozen and wind-burnt, with springtime dust blowing down the streets, and there's no leaves out yet, but the black-and-white film can't convey the red flags, carnations, and multicolored balloons, it just can't cope with the red, especially when there's so much of it. But maybe it's because of the music, which alternates between major and minor keys, but is invariably bold and brassy, rhythmic, square, like our buildings, like our city, sunny and dusty, a city of gleaming parallel tram tracks, of round public squares and arenas, of circus trombones. Of kettledrums, too.

(Hail to the peace-loving Leninist foreign policy of the Soviet Union! Hail to the great Soviet people!)

And here we have Palace Square, the stacked rows of the reviewing stand, functionaries in their fedoras, the huge round coat of arms wreathed in explosive gold ears of grain, and merry throngs of factory workers come pouring out from Neva Prospect as if from a horn of plenty, and they slow their pace and intermingle with other throngs while on the Hermitage facade a gigantic Lenin, who is also in a crowd of his own gigantic workers, strides out to meet us, as beaming children ride on their papas' shoulders, sitting on their creaky leather collars, blinking in the bright sun and waving toy flags above their papas' hats, bald spots, and haircuts, and by now the Komsomol girls from Shop Thirteen are tired of smiling so much at the fine young sailors, and the guests of honor, two process optimizers from Shop Thirty-One, have long been yearning to move on to the unofficial part of the celebration and wet their whistles, and the whole brass section is burning, too, with thirst and in the bright sun, and everyone's mouths are dry, and the asphalt has dried out, and the sun goes on scalding us from its official heavens—utterly white, round, bleached-out and arid—pouring onto our heads, our hats, the toy flags' round wooden dowel rods, the balloons and their strings clutched in little frozen fingers, and then the entire maniacal demonstration falls out of step and goes off course, heading slantwise out the corner of the screen, and all that's left is the empty square, bathed in cold May sunlight, as if from a fluorescent lamp, and now you must wait for December.

18.

The Theatergoer

Yes, absolutely! Film – that's absolutely right! says Director V encouragingly. That's exactly right. Please, help yourself! Mm-hmm. Yes. That's the spirit. Right! We don't quite have everything in what you'd call tip-top shape yet, and so we decided to invite you out. We may be looking at a new civilian order. A huge one. Medical. But they want to inspect the factory as part of the deal... and that's what I'm saying, inspect what? What for!? Better for us to make a film, see, than to have them go poking around all over the factory and—well, you know, just between us—bothering people who are trying to work! And we'll make a real good one for them, so good they'll want to place even more orders... Go on now, have some! No, sir, you are *not* driving today, either. Oh, and have some of this, our very own dear, esteemed W brought it back from London, he's our—Inga! Come in, come in! I'm not busy! As you can see, I like to do lots of things at once. I'm always available. You know what you should film first? Our new cafeteria! Absolutely! It was the first thing I redid when I assumed the position of director of this magnificent... Inga, the word "productivity" doesn't work here, it needs to be "performance," heh-heh... you get the difference, right? Look how it's all settled into place now. No chinks in the armor that way.

Because these days, it's not the quantitative indicators we're after... Well, let's go! Now feast your eyes on that! You see that? If you had to take a guess, what would you say that is? Hello? Yes, it's me, go on. No, send them to Fifteen, that's where everything is, and in mint condition, too! And now, where was I... those are picture tubes, cathode ray tubes. We made the CRTs for the very first Soviet televisions, and there were some extras hanging around the factory. It was my idea to line the stairwells with them. The design is just dazzling, don't you think? And do you see those lamps there? They were designed by the engineers of our EDB, honor and glory be to them! Oh, that's Experimental Design Bureau to you. And you might be thinking, well, *that's* nothing to brag about... but not so fast! Think of this, for example: here comes a worker out of his shop, and what does he see... Oh, Pal Palych! Hello! Come let me introduce you, this is the head of Shop Nine, his son also works here. I should add that he is also a close friend of my predecessor, the legendary Director N. Oh yes. Without N—I always say that without N we'd be... Did you know that in Latin, *gaudi* means "joy"? He's my favorite architect. Excuse me for just one minute. I already told you that I'm not signing until I get a look at a detailed draft. There's no fooling me. So. Can you get a close-up of me over here? Of me talking, and you just film it? Is the light good here? If it's not, we can render some assistance, we can utilize our pavilion, we have a... Ah, and this is our circuit-board assembly room! Greetings, comrades! The first thing I did when I came to the factory is automate everything. I have a passion for automation. Everyone else can go on worshipping heavy manual labor, but I'm not afraid to say it, I think that... well, I happened across the circuit-board assembly room and they near popped out of my head, my eyes, I mean! Women sitting there year after year, ruining their eyes placing and soldering all these tiny components by hand... So I go over to the EDB and I say, okay, who here is crazy enough to automate this? One guy steps up and says, I can. The Americans don't have anything like this! Please, help yourself, the head of Shop Thirty grows it himself in his own plot. Don't worry, it's all perfectly safe, we grow it ourselves right here outside our windows... no, no need to film that... As long as it's quick. Right. I understand. I understood it all perfectly well from the very beginning. No, we're going to build it as per the second option. Yes, regardless of the list. I haven't changed it, and I'm not going to change it anytime soon, either. Go ahead and film this, film us! These days it's not at all like it was back when N was here, of course; our objectives are different now. Primarily it's civilian manufacturing. We shouldn't get overly fixated on... you want to hear how they joke about me? "Our director's no old fart, his age is not a detriment; he has eagle eyes, a lion's roar, and Lenin's temperament." Haaa-ha-ha-ha! No, but I'm an fool, of course... Before Freedom I ran a factory in the city of Neybush. That's in the Yuryev oblast, it's practically in the Urals. We built a whole city there. Well, when I say *we*, I'm just... well, we built a factory, and several different residential districts on top of that, and a wastewater treatment plant, and schools and hospitals. And just what's going to happen if that factory stops? Did you ever think about that? Nobody thinks about that! We need to consider the larger system, first and foremost! This is the new mode of thinking, nobody in this country has thought like this before! If the factory stops, what will the workers do!? Now you can tell me all you like that it won't stop, but after all, sooner or later, there'll come a day when there won't be factories anymore! Well, I mean there will be a lot less of them. I read some studies... and just last night my wife and I were... Well!? You've got to be kidding! You can't go off all half-cocked like that! This is a tough one, you've got to ease it through. It takes delicacy. Try to nominate R, get him listed as a candidate. And then we'll see what happens, gauge their reaction. I'd consider this a good compromise. And so, yes, last night my wife and I were at the theater... and I should tell you that I'm an incurable theatergoer. When I was young I even thought I was going to be an actor. So yes, we get to the theater and it's a benefit for Gambrevsky. Now there's a whole story about that. Back in the day I was going to a technical school, but before I even finished it, I went to apply for a spot at the theater arts school, where he taught. This was all, my God, twenty-five years ago. So I went to see him. He tells me, everything's great, we'll take you. But they won't let me out of the technical school. They won't give me the piece of paper. Fine, says Gambrevsky. In that case, we'll accept you directly into the second year, so they can't keep you from going! So I go to see the dean of the school during his office hours, it was lucky that he had me... meaning, it was lucky for me that I had him... and he says, go on and see her, son... there was this actress back then, one Komarovskaya, she was older, an absolute genius... she spent a lot of time working with young people... and he says, go on and see her, I'll give you her phone number, and let her decide. So if she says that you should be an actor, then be one. I went to see her. We talked for about two hours. And she... If you know you shouldn't do something, then don't do it! Get the line repaired first, don't try to eyeball it and cobble something together yourself... So where was I. And Komarovskaya, she tells me: no, you shouldn't be an actor, you're ruled by your moods, an actor's life would kill you. And last night it was this whole story that I... Oh, now this you have to see. Out of all the innovations I'm trying to implement here at the factory, this one is my favorite. Management's going to be completely automated! All according to the Five-Year Plan's general line of automation and optimization! Imagine this: the entire production process is divided into operations, each one with an automatically designated manager, and each manager has a printer that spits out a piece of paper showing the timeline for completing the operation. Everything comes together, just like that. We're reducing the idle time between operations by thirty percent! I'm implementing it in September. Go ahead, keep filming… oh yes, and so after the show I go backstage to see Gambrevsky, and he recognizes me immediately! It's very strange, he says to me, it's very, very strange that you didn't become an actor! And I say to him, better a good general director than a bad actor! Ha-ha-ha! Don't you agree? I just have one very large favor to ask of you, folks. Turns out I'm showing off something awful here. I usually avoid that. But how else am I supposed to tell you about everything? I'm a fool, of course, but still… Yes! That's exactly right! Please, help yourselves!

19.

The Golden Globe

And here's a big one: cancer.

Hold off, don't flinch. What we're going to talk about now is how the Freedom Factory fought cancer across the entire Soviet Union. It's a true story, you can Google it if you want. It will be a story about a person by the name of X, a brilliant and insightful engineer as well as a man of rare genius, grace, and depth.

I had the pleasure of working with X (we'll name him after the X-ray) for forty years. I came here as a young woman, fresh out of the engineering institute, and I was assigned to the Golden Globe straightaway.

Back then, we were only just beginning to develop it. Director V had been seized by a powerful and secret desire to turn Freedom from a defense-industry factory into a civilian, non-military one. He was a believer, and he'd foreseen the future. I think V was every bit as good a director as the legendary N, although it's hard to compare them. And so, of his own accord, V made a proposal: give Freedom an order for machines that irradiate cancer patients! After all, we've already got the most important part: we know how to make precision sights! And let X work on it, he's so young, yet he's such a wonderful inventor, he always figures out the best solution on the fly, no matter what the problem.

And X did work on it. He put aside all his other projects, from then on concentrating only on the Golden Globe. He developed it himself, tested it himself, and got it into serial production himself, and he himself delivered and installed the first units.

Back then, there were no such machines in the USSR. There were ones with stationary mounts, where the head could slide up and down. But that meant that the patient had to be strapped down and rotated. Now the head on the Golden Globe could move in all directions. And that meant that you could calculate the precise dose, and not overradiate healthy tissue.

Remember Solzhenitsyn's *Cancer Ward*?

There's a scene where a seventeen-year-old girl is getting a mastectomy. It's hard to read about that. But Solzhenitsyn is a great writer, and later we read, "what her future child would now never do with that breast... ." In this way the author leads us to believe, to some extent, or at least to surmise, that the girl will survive, have a child, and nurse that child with the other breast.

So X and I, together we calmly got down to work on this issue, cognizant of how important it was, that it might even be the single most important issue in the Freedom Factory, as we had already privately concluded. As a manager, X was easygoing. Working with him was simple and easy. He never talked down to anybody. He could be sarcastic. But somehow it always turned out that everyone started working well, once they started working with him. Maybe he just knew how to assign every individual person exactly what that person could do best.

And X was also extremely sympathetic. Oncology is a difficult field. As soon as we began delivering our machines, there was a huge hullabaloo. The lines for radiation therapy were enormous. Then there were the bureaucratic hurdles, the bribes... but X knew everyone, you see. He had connections. And as soon as he heard that one of the workers had the disease, or someone in a worker's family, he would help them right away, get them set up with treatment. He'd go out personally to the clinics at Sandy Village or Birch Alley to make the arrangements.

On top of all that, he was a wit and an optimist, gallant around women, a marvelous raconteur; he loved to tell jokes, and he was an avid chess player; when it came down to it, he could even play a mean game of cards. And if you needed X during lunch, you just went to the EDB smoking room, where they'd have tournaments of blitz chess. But X didn't actually play any better than the others; there were better brains than his; it's just that it was pleasant to play with him, he was easygoing both about winning and about losing, so his competitor-slash-conversation partner enjoyed the game.

In addition, the boss was also possessed of a unique and brilliant talent for engineering. He'd often ask absolutely absurd questions, offer nonsensical suggestions, in order to draw people away from stereotypes and get them to look at things from a different angle. Then we'd start critiquing ideas, and then, all at once, the solution would fall right in our laps. There wasn't a single time when we couldn't figure out how to do something!

Our Golden Globe was a lifesaver for patients in Warsaw Pact countries. Although we supplied it to capitalist countries too. It's just that in the USSR, Bulgaria, Mongolia, Cuba, it was the only thing they had. Some Globes are thirty, forty years old now, but they still work, they're still saving people's lives. It's true that you do have to replace the cobalt on time, and people don't always do that... but there were problems with the cobalt back then, sometimes, too... the machine would be installed, let's say, but there wasn't any cobalt for it yet. Once X went to a clinic in Georgia for an installation, and he sees patients sitting in line in the hallway leading to the shielded treatment room with the Golden Globe. They've got their pullets in baskets, they've got their wine, and so forth… and X inquires with the lead doctor to find out what's going on, since, after all, there's still no cobalt in the machine! And the man tells him, all condescending: "But you see, my friend: it's psychotherapy!"

All jokes aside, though, there's some truth to it. Some patients want to get more radiation. But you can't do that. So you give them an appointment for a radiation session without radiation. Just as a demonstration. I have no idea whether it helps. But if the sick person's less afraid, that's already something.

There was another time, in another southern city: we were doing a radiation survey, checking the operating conditions. We find out that the radiation level is surging on the street behind one of the walls. X says, we can't allow this. Build a shielded room. The head doctor shoots back, "Look, maybe I just post a guard, to chase people away?"

But that tradition, of helping the factory workers and their families if they get sick, is still going strong. When my mom got cancer, they got her set up with radiotherapy right away. Although even the Golden Globe couldn't help her.

You might be getting the impression that X lived a carefree, easygoing life, but that's not quite the way it was. He still ended up… after years of working in this field, he still… especially as the years went on, he… I don't quite know how to put it. I'll just tell you what happened, although I'm not sure it's worth it.

X had many acquaintances, but two close friends. One was a sociologist, the other an anthropologist. I don't know where they are now, or whether they're still alive. The three of them—X and those two—developed a strange and frightening hypothesis. And keep in mind that this wasn't just the fruit of idle thoughts, as they say. There was a scientific basis, there was proof. These days, you don't hear about this hypothesis. X eventually stopped working on it, and never published anything on it.

I worked in very close proximity to X, but I never asked about this hypothesis of theirs. Just one time, at New Year's, it was New Year's, 1988, and we were bringing it in with X at his dacha, he and I were sitting on his veranda around five o'clock in the morning, the snow was glittering outside the windows, we were smoking, drinking coffee, and freezing, and I gathered up my courage and asked, that hypothesis the three of you developed, what was it? And X laid it all out for me, very matter-of-factly. In plain language, this is what they discovered: humanity is like a cancerous disease. Humanity is a cancer. It develops according to the very same laws. It attacks itself, and even though it's fighting, it's doomed. X backed it up with lots of proof, I don't remember it all now. But he proved it to me.

So I said, but what about God? I don't know why, but that's the question I put to him. I asked, is that really the most important thing, the main thing about us—that we attack ourselves? X says to me, no. That's not the most important thing. But he says it to me in such a way that I realize: it doesn't matter that it's not the most important thing. It still doesn't contradict their hypothesis. We cut the dragon's head off, but three more grow in its place. And this isn't just the resistance of cancer, or bacteria. He was talking about humanity itself, about human reason, civilization.

I found out much later that X had had problems because of this hypothesis. Even though he'd never even tried to publish it. Small wonder. It's a terrifying hypothesis, hopeless. But now you see—right?—who X was, what he did his whole life. Knowing how it fit into the big picture, knowing what was really behind it all, he still spent his whole life making more and more of his Golden Globes, saving millions of lives. Maybe I shouldn't have told you. But without knowing this, it wouldn't make sense. And knowing this, everything falls into place.

20.

Optimizations

At our factory, everybody's a process optimizer. The director encourages it. If you come up with some kind of new lug or weldolet, go ahead and use it. He's a process optimizer himself, our Director V is. In spirit. That's the way we are, here at Freedom. From the cleaning ladies or interns to the director, we all of us apply optimizations. And we don't just come up with them, we share them with each other. You guys want our invention? Go right ahead! Take it and implement it.

But what about me? I also came up with a dozen or so lugs and weldolets and whatnot, but eventually I got tired of it. You know what I mean. What I wanted in the long run was to settle the whole issue, once and for all. Because what is the most important thing in a factory? You think it's machines, right? Equipment? Not even close. The most important thing we have is people. But that's exactly where it's hellooo-oo, process optimizers, where are you? Nothing. Nobody's doing anything along these lines. Everybody's trying to perfect the machine. You get you some drills, sure, some new milling cutters, but what about the human being, hmm? Aha, you see?

So that's how I decided to work along those lines, because I have a natural inclination for that kind of thing. I got my cousin to stop smoking, as an example. I didn't rub it in his face, I didn't propagandize him or show him smokers' lungs. He wouldn't've cared, anyway. All I did was I said, quit! Either quit, or annex Kamchatka. So my cousin thought about it for a while, got the wheels turning, and—Kamchatka'd be harder. So he quit smoking. Switched to meat pies. His wife makes them for him.

But at the factory, it's not that easy. It's a whole different ball of wax. The people here are the real deal, genuine factory-welded construction. Take F, for example, the head of Shop Seventeen. Big, strong guy. Tosses back a glass of the hard stuff every night after work. For him, it's just like breathing, doesn't do a thing for him. You don't get drunk from air, do you? Just in extreme cases. Same thing with smoking. He lights his next one off the first. No good trying to come at him from that angle. But if you bring in the chakras, it works.

I've got this book at home. Well, you wouldn't quite call it a book, exactly, it's more just photocopied pages. But don't go thinking it's not—that author did publish a book. But just one. It sold out fast, and you know yourself how things are with reprints here. Not on the top of the priorities list. There was a whole lot there. It talked about cold-water showers, and going barefoot, and how water remembers everything, and about wood ears and shark teeth. And it also talked about blood irradiation. Now it's true that that part was more speculative, the author himself specified that he hadn't actually tried it, since—where exactly was he supposed to go to try it? But the author was strongly convinced that if you irradiated your blood it'd be enormously beneficial to your entire body, you'd be healthier, and you'd live to a hundred and ten, on average, depending on your individual potency. So that was the part that I picked up on.

I'm a modest person. So quiet-like, without going on about myself and my record of accomplishments, I implemented my optimization proposal on myself and a few of my comrades in Nine, that's the fab shop. Kolya told his wife, and some of the accountants joined in (three ladies from the cost accounting section). So we found a little side room and started irradiating our blood during our lunch break. The first thing we did was pool our money for a big crystal platter at the Narva department store. We bought it to make everything nice, aesthetically pleasing, which is not unimportant. And also to increase the surface area being irradiated. It's harder to do that in, say, a saucepan, or a jug. Then we finagled an IV drip from Anton A's sister, she was a head nurse in the infectious diseases ward of the children's clinic over on Avant-Garde Street. And we got down to business. We put some of our blood out into the platter, irradiated it, and then put it back in. We didn't forget the difference in blood types, and we never mixed incompatible types. Although we didn't have any of those, anyway. Due to a happy coincidence, almost all of us were A-positive blood types. Nikolay's wife was the only one who was different, but hers was O, which everybody knows can be transfused to people with all the other blood types.

A word about the results. It goes without saying that I kept a record of the experiment. The very first month after implementing my optimization, the project participants' aggregate productivity increased by 43%, even if you include Grisha, who went on a drinking binge at the end of the month. And if you eliminate Grigory, then our aggregate productivity went up by more than 70% in the first month! That's almost twice as much! Of course we can't rule out the influence of other factors, such as seasonal variations, but we couldn't exactly have a control group, and we needed time to do more research. But we didn't get that time, alas. The forty-seventh day after initiating the implementation of my optimization proposal, one of the enterprise security service folks walks into our room. He says, "Are you out of your fucking minds, people? You want to end up in the morgue?" and takes away the platter, the IV drip, and the radiation machine, without even giving us a chance to put the blood back into our bodies. So just like that he confiscated not only our equipment, but also our blood, blood that we still could've gotten a lot of use out of.

We were all pretty dejected. My letters of explanation didn't change a thing. Every time somebody mentioned my optimization proposal, Pavel Pavlovich P, the head of our shop, cursed up a blue streak and yelled at me. The gist of his narrative was that I should experience positive emotions that I still had my job at Freedom, that I still had my freedom at all. Then I was finally able to get in to see Lev Ilych V, the director. He heard my whole story through to the end, busted out laughing, slapped me on the shoulder, and said, good job! Keep up the good work! So I went back to work.

Maybe my optimization proposal really wasn't suitable for an enterprise like ours. I decided not to fixate on it, and started developing a chessboard where the pieces move by themselves, so you can play chess on the ceiling.

21.
Trout

Tanechka, who used to be the chief dispatcher, but now is head of the labor union, is headed out with the chief economist and production planner, O, to get the trout. I have so much to do, the insurance was due yesterday, but can you really say no to our dear director? Yes, V is strange. Is that really a job for the chief economist, driving out to a private fish pond for some fish? What do we even need this trout for, anyway? Just between you and me, I think it's a pretty risky venture. We should've raised beef cattle or kept bees instead. Oh, don't even talk to me about bees. (Kingisepp Highway, empty and straight as an arrow.) Did you know that V really is planning on setting up apiaries? Although I think it'll never get past the planning stages. Not necessarily. People will say, oh, so we'll also get to have bees… Tanechka, but that was great, though! How'd you pull that off? You got a medical allowance for all the employees. It was sheer delight to watch you do it. A room full of gray-haired generals, and here comes this, you know, little slip of a girl and cuts right to the chase: if the managers are getting their hundred percent full salary, then pay the line workers their fifty percent! And… deathly silence… Ah, well, I regretted being so blunt. I should've put it more gently. No, Tanechka, gently doesn't do it. You got it just right. Just right.

Nobody else knew what was really going on, and what was riding on it, that's all. But I know. Don't be afraid. You're still young enough to not be afraid.

They had to all but physically force me into the labor union, actually. Did you know that I have a degree in philology? Yes, that's right. There was a point where I really needed to get out of the city, for family reasons, just to cut myself off from everything. So I went on a business trip to the Crimea, where there were some sea trials. The very first day I was there, I almost drowned. Can't you just see it? My friend and I had waded into the sea and started swimming. I wasn't used to it, I hadn't gone swimming in three years, so my arms and legs started cramping up. So I say, totally calmly: Lyusya, I'm drowning! Good thing we still hadn't had a chance to swim out very far… is it all right that I'm telling you all this? It's more than all right that you're telling me all this, Tanechka.

Hello, hello, hello! Oh, my, look what upper-level management we have visiting today! So then, let's go get everything written up. Ivan Dmitrych, please pass on an enormous thank-you to your engineers, and especially to comrade H himself, for the fish feed spreader! Is there any way you all could think up some other piece of equipment that can catch and load the fish? Ask them, please! You can do anything, I know it! Ivan Dmitriyevich… um, excuse me, what's your name? Aaahh, the labor union! I'm honored. Here, this is for you. I… thank you. How do you… what do you do with trout? Eat it? To tell the truth, no. You exchange it. For cheaper fish. Cod is ten kilograms to one. Whitefish is three. You salt it, put it up for winter. Otherwise, we sell it to restaurants. As usual. But isn't this fine! Isn't this lovely! Now we'll be needing an hour, hour and a half, to… but you can go for a walk in the meantime, for example, you could go over to our river, we

have some very picturesque hills there. Meanwhile we'll do the catching and weighing.

The day is very quiet, gray, dark, subdued. The riverbank falls off into quiet, clear water. Gray stones lie scattered about. The gray-green grass is all dried up. It's amazing how quiet and warm it is here. You'd never know it'll be winter soon. Hey, let's have a fire! But how do we… what do we build it with? We're in a field, after all. We'd have to go find some sticks… Never mind, you're right, let's not.

And here's the water. It looks like walls are towering over the water. Do you have any favorite poems, Ivan Dmitriyevich? Me? Oh, I don't know any poems at all. I have an abominable memory for poetry. And a very good one for figures. Well, that makes sense. What about you, Tanechka? You know, there was this English poet, William Blake. I've heard the name. You read him in the original, I take it? I tried to translate him myself. It's very difficult. Here's one I tried: *Then come home my children, the sun is gone down / And the dews of night arise / Your spring and your day are wasted in play / And your winter and night in disguise.* Why'd you pick such a sad one? Let's have you stand on that stone over there, this one is tippy. Don't be scared. That's it.

Tanechka, I've wanted to go somewhere with you for a long time. Anywhere. You're an amazing person. (Damn it, damn it, damn it! What am I saying?! An amazing person! I might as well have said "an amazing little person!" Or "I'm single, and you're single!" I can't imagine anything more inept than that!!) Me? Amazing? Ivan Dmitriyevich, I'm an awkward person. To this day I still don't know what I want from myself. I'm a silly fool, Ivan Dmitriyevich. Ah, I'm a fool too. I criticize everyone. I make fun of everyone. I can't make myself stop. Me too. I only see a series of deficiencies. As though I were underlining mistakes with a red pen. I should've gone ahead and been a teacher. But people, they're actually completely different, you know. People are totally different! Everyone has that somewhere deep down inside, don't they? If they didn't, Tanechka, we wouldn't do so much evil in the world. All the evil we do is because of what we have deep down inside us. We want to feel nice, and good, so we do evil. Yes, that's true. I've cried so much because of that. That labor union committee has cost me so many tears... it's only now that I... don't feel quite so despicable because of every little thing... *You* cried?! But you are so cheerful! So sunny! Yes. When Konstantin Ivanovich was alive, I'd go running to him. I'd run over to him, have a little cry... Who do you cry to now? Now I... Ivan Dmitriyevich, who is that up there, waving his arms? Oh, that moron. What makes you say he's a moron? Everything. Has it really been an hour and a half already? He probably finished a lot earlier. He's increased his productivity. You're being mean. Me? No, Tanechka. Just the opposite. I'm glad. I don't like driving after dark. Tanechka, do you know why he's a moron? Because he's going to end badly. Now, really. Do you think so? I know so. He's a petty thief. And he's going to end badly. When this whole damned... planned economy... goes to the dogs (they're panting as they clamber hand-in-hand up the hill)... he'll be the first one shot... Ivan Dmitriyevich!! Ah, to hell with it. He grits his teeth and yanks on Tanechka's arm. Startled, she yelps, Oh! and rushes after him. Here's your fish, my esteemed friends. Well, how was your walk? How did you enjoy your time? How did you like our local color?

What'd you go out there for, you idiot? Director V asks O the next day. What did you go out there for? Idiot. What do you think I sent you both out there for? Do you think I sent you out there for the *fish*? Hopeless! O shrugs and sidles edge-wise out of the office.

22.

The BITC Dispatch System

My esteemed comrade dispatchers! My name is Ivan Aryefich C. I'm a supervisory engineer in the Experimental Design Bureau of Factory 85, the Freedom Factory, which produces radioeletronic equipment. Today I have the privilege of presenting to you our joint project, an invention we developed and implemented at our factory. Comrades, this is our civilian system, the BITC Dispatch System, which stands for Basic Integrated Technical Control Dispatch System. It will allow us to increase the operational productivity of our housing and public utilities department. We are all aware, comrades, that this department's work leaves something to be desired, but this is not because of any one individual's bad intentions. This is because it's not automated enough. Our general director, comrade V, has prioritized the automation of everything, including the civilian population. My esteemed comrade dispatchers! What you see before you is the console of the BITC Dispatcher. Here we have the indicator lights for forty buildings in our district, running from left to right. And all those buildings have elevators, comrades. You'll get an audio signal if someone is trying to contact you from an elevator that's stuck. Down below we have additional indicators. These ones here are for fires. As soon as there's a fire in a building, the BITC Dispatcher System signals you. It might just be that in your district there's no gas, all the stoves are electric, but we do also have monitoring for gas leaks, those indicators are right over here. And unlike the other indicators, which are red, these are blue. And so, you're sitting here, and something starts blinking. What do you do? Right. You don't have to run off anywhere. You just call. Either that, or you'll get a call yourself, at the console. You pick up the receiver and you hear, "elevator number such-and-such, building such-and-such." And you sit here comfortably and call out the repair crew. The BITC Dispatcher unit is extremely simple to use, and allows you to regulate and monitor all housing problems. Other districts of the city that are going to be equipped with our unit include South-West, Kupchino, Kolpino, Peterhof, Avtovo, Okhta, Dybenko, and others. Are there any questions, my esteemed comrade dispatchers? No questions. Thank you!

My esteemed comrade dispatchers! My name is Ivan Aryefich C! I'm the supervisory engineer of the Freedom radio-electronics factory. Our Director V thinks that I and I alone, the inventor of the system in question, can describe its advantages and disadvantages better than anybody else. Earlier today I visited your colleagues in Kupchino and they really liked our system, they asked a whole lot of questions. What you see before you is the console of the BITC Dispatch System, which stands for Basic Integrated Technical Control Dispatch System, which will allow us to increase the operational productivity of our housing and public utilities. This system has proven its productivity in the course of prototype testing... I'll be brief: what you see before you is a console! You're going to be using this console in the course of your day-to-day work, so I advise you to completely memorize it! These little blinking lights up here along the top are showing you that an elevator is stuck. You can go on ahead and write down the

number of the one that actually got stuck. If you hear an audio signal, it means you're getting an incoming call from the
stuck elevator. Once I got stuck in an elevator myself. I know
how unpleasant it is. But at least I got stuck with a whole
shopping bag of food and a pleasant female companion. Actually, it was an unforgettable experience. Getting stuck's not
that bad… Well. And so here you have the gas indicators, but
they'll only work depending on where they are, so I'm not
sure you'll need them. And then here we have the indicators
that are specially designated for fires. Ha-ha! The tiniest whiff
of smoke, let's say some kids are smoking marijuana on the
staircase, and boom! She goes off! Ha, take that! Sorry. Let's
say you're sitting here, and it starts blinking. What do you
do? That's right, you don't have to run around! You can just
make a call! So you sit here in comfort and call out the repair
crew. Several districts of the city are equipped with our unit,
including South-West, Kupchino, Kolpino, Peterhof, Avtovo,
Okhta, Dybenko, and others. Do you have any questions, my
esteemed dispatchers? That's what I thought. Thank you!

My esteemed comrade dispatchers! My name is Ivan
Aryefich C, but to hell with that, you can just call me Aryefich. I invented this thing here… well, I mean, I've invented
a lot of stuff, but this thing will save everybody. As long as
nobody steals the copper cable, that is. I'm really worried
that somebody's going to run off with that copper cable. If
that happens, this stupid thing won't even work, so you have
to make sure nobody takes it. People have gotten really bad
these days… It's called the BITC Dispatch System… I know,
I laughed too… I invented it, but I didn't name it. We have a
special design department. Our director's a psycho. But who's
not a psycho in this world, right? You're the third place I've
been to today, so please excuse me… However, enough with
the introductions! This is the console! As you can see there

are these little bitty lights here that blink at you, so tenderly, in different colors. Right now this console means nothing to you, but in time you'll see it for what it is. So right here is if an elevator gets stuck. And it depends where. And if somebody calls, pick up right away. This here is if there's a fire. Now that's no joke. If that happens you've got to call somebody out right away, even if it's just that somebody's burned their pancakes. When people start going and getting drunk, anything can catch fire! People just go and leave their cigarette butts lying around... You think I didn't put myself heart and soul into this?! I'm just afraid that this damn thing is going to break down like it always does! And what's it to you? You don't give a crap! You're just going to turn it off and walk away! But I'm here to appeal to you: don't turn it off! Just stay sitting there in the dispatcher's office, what's so hard about that? But just watch out for the little lights! Keep your eye on them! And that was my show for today. I'm off, I've still got one more district to go!

Gentlemen, as our director likes to say... he's completely nuts, but he wants to serve the people! I'm Aryefich... So these are lights here! You've got your fires, your gas leaks, and your stuck elevators... Somebody's definitely gonna walk off with your copper cable, people're gonna steal every last little thing, but don't you pay any attention, you just go ahead and keep working, I love all of you, I really do... I have two hundred and twenty patents... I was born in a clearing in the woods, you know, way out in the middle of nowhere... and now here I am making consoles for sixteen-story buildings... forty buildings... and it's all right here, the little lights are blinking, see? Our factory works for death, for defense, and I'm the only one, well, and our own dearly beloved comrade X, who makes machines to fight cancer, we're the only ones who work for life! But what can you do? Dispatchers! I'm appealing to you to… They promised to give me a Zhiguli if I can get it adopted and implemented! I already got my driver's license! Elevators get stuck, buildings catch fire, gas leaks explode! It's in our power to prevent all that!! Let's drink to it, comrades! And again, let's drink again… Kupchino and Okhta, Obukhovo and Neva, Vasilyev and Kronstadt, let's all drink together to our dispatcher's console! She's a real BITCH! Ivan Aryefich, no more for you, you've had enough!

23.

Wild Strawberries, Bittersweet

I'm running along a slippery pine plank. The soles of my gym shoes are white rubber, the pattern of their prints is stars and snowflakes in relief. I'm running along a thin path in bleached-out shadows, through a hash of leaves, shadows, and light. My legs are dew-drenched from the knee down. I give the baton to M, the team tosses her onto a rope, she grabs another one strung above it and slides along, pulling herself farther and farther away. C, a design engineer, is nibbling pensively on a downy white dandelion. The sun is shining down through the pines. There's the scent of pine and wind, water and wild strawberries, sand and resin.

We're in a skiff. I dip my hand overboard into the water, the cool water parts and burbles, flows through my fingers, splashes and sprays. The finishing engineer K (that's me), sunglasses on, lounges in the stern with a cigarette in his mouth. The shore is steep, sandy, piney. I take my sunglasses off and everything looks bleached-out, bright-white, hot; and I smell the scent of the sun-warmed skiff, and I see girls, and shards of sunny water, and the refractory depths, and droplets on my belly; I want to go for a swim; I stand on the heavy, rocking edge of the boat and dive, the girls squeal, I dive deep, noisily. The water is rippling, transparent; the lake's been poured all the way up to the sky, to my ears, to the tops of the pine trees, to the back of my head... it's fresh water, clean, bubbly, the spilled oil of the sun spreading over it. We're on the shore, and M is standing in a blueberry patch, in a blue-black blueberry patch, in the red-brown shadows cast by spruces and pines, M and her red hair, young M, with her ripe, round, freckled shoulders, her lips dark with blueberries, an ant is running up my leg, M is dappled in light and shadows, and a downy nimbus of fine, light-red hair glows around her head. Ridges of sand lie at the bottom of the shallow water, in rippling patches of shade and light; the blinding, flashing water stretches far out into the distance; they're waving at us from the skiff; I sense that I might wake up at any moment, so I make an effort, pushing at the resonant water with my arms and legs, and I remain on the surface of sleep.

We've all settled in next to each other, all six of us, in an almost motionless dance, R fanning himself with a pair of fins, while K, in back (oh yes, that's me), fans himself with a pair of shorts, but J is lying face-up, her head thrown back languorously, thrusting her small bikini cups up to the sun, and next to her M, in an unintentionally effective pose, is nibbling on a cucumber, L is lying spread-eagled with her face shaded by a large burdock leaf, and hot-tempered F, right in the middle, sits in lotus position with a dark smile, a towel around his neck and a newspaper over his head, the newspaper looks completely white, in the sun you can't see the letters, we've settled in right where the sun is beating down hardest, we're wet, over there in the shade is a bottle made of dark glass, and everything's moving in slow-motion with furious speed, we're lazing like scalded cats, and the space around us vibrates, it trembles with laziness, passion, and the languid summer day. Now F in his newspaper hat, with his dark, haughty face and medieval squint, is warmed up, and M has eaten almost the whole cucumber, and J doesn't move while the sun bakes her, but it's leaving the explosive putty filling the black-and-white cups wet and white, and K slowly, furiously waves his shadow-laced fan, while R fans with his fins, which are gradually drying; and the air thunders, and the sun flashes, but L and J are stock-still, and the tops of the pines are stock-still, and only the living black lake water melts, refractory, unwilling, it moves, shifts, and glitters; only the rippling water, which looks like light, trembles, evaporating into the thick, deep-blue vault of the sky, the alarm clock wants me to wake up, but I'm not having it, not on your life.

The sack races, at first K keeps up, jumping along a sandy volleyball court, but then he hits his head on the net, doubles over, falls down, and rolls in the sand, in his sack, and Romka stretches out his hand with a little toy, a doll, and the girls laugh, and not having to jump anymore feels so good to K that he's not even in a hurry to get up, and how is it that some people want to win, he thinks, but me, I don't want anything, I don't want to go anywhere, I feel good just like this, I'm in such a stupor, never mind that hot-tempered F in his sack nimbly hopped away to his nowhere, to the finish line, with mighty thrusts of his blue-black, veiny legs, black F, but I don't want to go anywhere; there it is, the balancing point, it's where the birdie is stuck in the red pine branches over the net, it's where the volleyball flew off to, it's where the red campfire licks sunny rocks, and over them is a young M, and my vision's going dark from the light, and I don't want to go back to anywhere, but I'm already waking up in soft white vales, the streetlight is shining into the room through semi-transparent green shades, someone is scraping at the snow with a metal shovel, our whole room is dark and penetratingly illuminated, I'm lying on my back in white soft vales, I'm just about to wake up and return to my sixty-seven years, but my awakening keeps on going.

A young M tosses her downy head and lays out a green map on her knees, clad in tight gym pants. The map is rippling, it's pale green with pale blue streams and dotted bogs. It's partly cloudy over the map, half the map is in shade, half in the sun. Metal spoons reflect blinding rays. *The deep-green shadowed evening's chased our day away, and fleet upon my lips, the summer's taste: wild strawberries, bittersweet.*

24.

Radiation Detector

So that's the deal, says the chairman of the radiation control committee. It's up to us. He looks at the clock. The clock shows four-thirty AM. The director of the Freedom Factory springs out of his chair and runs across the office to the window, where he peers out at the trees in agitation. But there'll be trains coming in, he said musingly. And airplanes. And trucks. And steamships. Have they all gone fucking nuts there, or what? **** Soviet power, ****. Did they even think about this at all? The chairman of the audit and oversight committee chuckles softly. Did they think, he says. Yes… thinking… that's not their cup of tea. Hasn't been for a long while. Did you know that five days after the explosion, Kiev went out for its May Day demonstration? Complete with children and pregnant women… and meanwhile everybody in Europe is hiding in bunkers… but all we did is evacuate Pripyat… and now it's the same thing, of course, they're not thinking again. They couldn't care less that all of Leningrad's going to be eating radioactive apples and blue—but now they remember! It's the end of August! The school year's right around the corner, the kids'll be coming back from the Crimea… Anyway, this is the deal, Lev Ilych. We have one week. Can you come up with something? What am I going to come up with, Vova? What? We're a military factory. Yes, yes, I know that. I know.

But just—something. To protect the city, at least a little. Director V: what about a radiation detector? A small, portable radiation detector. At one point there were talks about it, right after the accident itself, back in June. But I didn't encourage it. There was no budget for it. And now, we have a week left. Do we even have any draft designs? No. Have to build it from scratch. It'll never happen, Lev Ilych. Let's try. What do we have to lose? We'll try. And we'll do it. So, shall we make a revolution, Vova? We shall, Lev Ilych. And just like the Gerondins, you and I will be the first to get our heads chopped off. Let's get to work.

Let's get to work, agrees Director V. He picks up the phone and calls the Chief Engineer, H, at home. My esteemed colleague, says director V, his voice soft and wan. Get ready to go. The motherland is calling. Chief Engineer H betrays not the slightest hesitation: what are we making? A radiation detector, replies V. Thank God! cries H. You scared me. What, you've had worse? I have, confirms H. Okay. A portable radiation detector? The EDB has to be ready in two days for us to have enough time to implement production and make the first batch. Call everybody in.

Easy to say it "has to be ready." But this isn't just knocking together the production line for the latest series. It's not like back when F slapped together four Mimosas for the November 7th holiday. This time you've got to sit down first and figure out what you're going to do. It's a new thing that has never before existed, anywhere on earth. Sure, there were some ideas. In H's head. But that's all. And it's a long road from raw idea to finished model. We have to reach the end of that road in two and a half days.

And we do. The concept is ready by morning (H called a meeting to resolve the main issues of portability and reliability). The algorithms have been developed. The rest of the day is devoted to developing the technical drawings. By the evening of the first day, the drafters have begun their work. By the next morning, the radiation detector is ready, on paper. That's one day.

And a good thing, too, that it only took one day. Because the prototype is also made in the EDB. It's made there, then it's tested in trial production, and only after that does it go into line production at the factory. And you can't skip a single step here. No matter how insanely urgent it is, you can't skip anything. The prototype is produced in special shops that only work for the EDB. The end of the workday is nowhere in sight. The prototype is finished by three in the morning on the second day, and by eleven AM it's been tested. There it is, there's our radiation detector, everybody pay attention. It can measure the background radiation. It can let you know whether your cargo is okay. What are you carrying, life or death? It's the yes or no game all over again: do you have any brothers or sisters… But oh, what's riding on the result. Two days and counting. So far so good.

So now it's time to figure out how to put it into line production. It's better to lose a whole day on that, because then you'll make it up in five minutes. If you don't figure this out, then it was all for nothing. And the person who has to figure it out is the head of Shop Seventeen. His technicians help him. How can you make this piece here, the one that you already have one of, and make it fast? So fast that in five days you can turn one into one hundred? Make that in four days, because you already spent one whole day figuring it all out, but nobody's blaming you for that, since one day is so little, and the fact that you were able to get everything lined up by midnight is a major victory.

So right away, right at that same midnight, the shops get down to work. A hundred radiation detectors in four days is a whole lot. One hundred of the best and most reliable devices, capable of determining the radiation level in a train car or cargo hold. And this is just for starters, because then we'll need more, after all we still have Moscow and Nizhnyy Novgorod to go, and even Novosibirsk… all the places where they'll be sending airplanes with radioactive food from Belorussia and Ukraine. They're not thinking. It's our job to think. So we will think about the problem, and we will think about the solution, and we will work, just plain work, the eyes are afraid but the hands do the work. And our hands *do* do the work. A hundred radiation detectors are done in six and a half days, and they're all shipped out in time for the first day of school, the first of September, they're distributed to all the coast guard stations, all the ports, all the train stations and railroads. Everywhere.

And then Director V—who didn't come home from the factory at all the whole time, who spent the whole week in his office because he doesn't know how to run around the factory from shop to shop, like Director N, although he does know how to run around his office, which he does extremely well and to great effect—Director V gets a call from Moscow. A loud, jangling voice asks, can you do that again… in a week… for us, too? The lot we need's a little bigger… four hundred units… can you do it?

At that, Director V takes quite a large amount of air into his lungs, but he senses that the world is too big, he can't inhale all the air there is, he can't fit it all inside him. So then he presses his console's call button: Simochka, please put me through to chief engineer H. Hurry, now. He's probably sitting around somewhere putting his feet up…

25.

The Factory Comedy Troupe

Greetings and salutations, esteemed Earthlings, guests of our planet! You're looking around in amazement... don't you know where you've ended up? Wait, wait, no: you have *no idea* where you've ended up. So here's where: you are in the Freedom Factory. Shhhh! Talking about freedom is forbidden. But what is "freedom," exactly? It's when your boss says, "That's it, no need to show up at work anymore!" You fool, that's not freedom. Freedom is when YOU can say, "That's it, no need to show up at work anymore!"

Wow! So what's this you've got here? It's a milling machine. It makes parts. All by itself? Well, almost. Our machines are computerized. How does it work? Um... I don't know. He doesn't know how I'm constructed, folks! Then I don't have to know how it's constructed, either. Still, we both have a lot in common. It likes lots of grease. And I like lots of grease, too. That's why we're still together after all this time, me and my machine. The director shot a film about my typical workday, and now he shows that film diligently and promptly at my workstation, every day, while me and my machine, why, we just kick back and down our grease.

But what are these parts actually for? Shhhh! Talking about that is forbidden. We used to hide the fact that we make submarine equipment, but now we hide the fact that we no longer make it. We're good at hiding things. Sometimes we hide a thing so well that later we forget where we put it. We even forget what it was. For example, there was this one instrument called the—shhhh! The point is, we assembled it with our eyes closed. We assembled it, mounted it, pushed the launch button, and that's all, folks! Nothing left standing. The end of the world, right? So the finishers had to fine-tune the settings a little. And we ended up with a perfectly marvelous electric meat grinder.

As a matter of fact, right now we're in the middle of the conversion process. That means that instead of making rockets, we're going to be making washing machines. What? You think those aren't very scary? Our washing machines are scarier than any bomb! Our bombs don't explode, but our washing machines do. Regularly! The only thing that could possibly be worse than a hostile nuclear era is a peaceful atomic age.

Incidentally, who is making that terrible racket over there? Oh, that! That's our very own Pal Palych P, eating some bread and salami. But why's it grating and grinding so loud? Well, because the salami's strong as steel. It's also produced by a former defense industry factory. Like we said: conversion.

But still, why the god-awful grinding? Well, because Pal Palych is also strong as steel. He's gotten so steely because our dear Operations Director F is always tempering him. Calls him into the office and gives him a talking-to, blows that liquid nitrogen all over him. Pal Palych comes out and looks almost alive for the rest of the day.

Working in Freedom has gotten hard, so hard. It used to be easier. You didn't come to work? A bullet. You didn't make the deadline? A bullet. But not now. Now we're converted. You didn't come to work? Into the meat grinder. You didn't make the deadline? Into the meat grinder.

The only place everything's the same as always is back in the galvanizing shop. It's still the good old days in there. The same good old tanks of sulfuric acid. The same good old green fog in the air. And the same good old Vera Mikhaylovna B. Oh! My esteemed Vera Mikhaylovna! We held a referendum on you. The issue was posed in the following way: "Vera Mikhaylovna: good for you or bad for you?" Unfortunately, we can't publicize the results of the referendum, because in the interest of maintaining secrecy, Margarita Konstantinovna ate the piece of paper documenting the results right after reading it. Since she was not poisoned as a result, we concluded that Vera Mikhaylovna is good for you, not bad for you. Thank you, Vera Mikhaylovna, for all your hard work!

As for our very own Director V… well, when it comes to him, plain prose is simply inadequate to the task. So we wrote a song about him.

You should have seen by the look in my eyes, Director
There was a part missin'
You should have known by the tone of my voice, maybe
But you didn't listen
The engineers played dead,
but you forged ahead
making mixers, not missiles,
you went ahead and changed the mission

And though I know all about those machines
that are due in November,
You gotta give us, Director, the plans way before then,
So we can put 'em together
And I meant
Every word I said
When I said this'll take overtime,
I meant it won't be ready, ever—

And I'm gonna keep on millin' screws
'Cause it's the only thing I want to do
I don't want to sleep,
I just want to keep on millin' screws

And I meant
Every word I said
When I said that I love my job, I meant it,
please don't send me away forever

And I'm gonna keep on millin' screws
'Cause it's the only thing I want to do
I don't want to sleep,
I just want to keep on millin' screws…

But all this is mere lyricism. It's actually easy to sleep in Freedom! It's working that's hard. See, the order forms are too short: you run out of room by the sixteenth time you have to change the production schedule for your part. But in this case, the solution is simple: simply flip the order form, and there! You've started afresh, turned over a new leaf! The main thing is not to let F see you doing this. Otherwise he'll make you take it orally. Meaning, to be administered by mouth. Although there's another option. You could also take it recta— ahem! But why dwell on the negative, friends. On the whole, our F is nice. He's just kind of… polar… by nature. Speaking of which, too bad Director N didn't let him go to the Antarctic way back when. We'd have apple orchards growing there by now. But as it is, we've had to establish the South Pole right here in Freedom. We even have our own emperor penguins: as soon as our shop foremen catch sight of F, they huddle together and hunch over to protect their little guys.

At least our director has taken pains to make sure that everything's optimized here in Freedom! That means that while you used to get away with doing shoddy work, now you can work worse than ever before! And if you used to work well, then now you see there's no way the work's ever getting better, so you quit working altogether.

But to tell the truth, none of the aforementioned disadvantages bother us a bit! What would our planet be without Freedom? It would be some kind of provincial Pluto! Who'd mow the hay and dig up the potatoes if it weren't for our engineers? Who'd raise the trout? Not to mention all that other little stuff, like navigational instruments and radiation therapy machines... Basically, without Freedom, you lose track of the most basic things: What time is it? Where are my pants? Who am I? Everyone who's ever worked for Freedom has experienced this for themselves. On weekends. Freedom disciplines us, somehow. Would you like to stay with us forever, esteemed aliens? It's almost the same here with us as it is on Earth. What tasty radioactive apples grow out by Building Four! And how strong the tanks of sulphuric acid are! Stay with us, or there won't be anybody here to do the work! Did you know that in Freedom, every single person can be of use? Not even philologists can tear themselves away from us! They curse in every language known to man, but they don't leave. And what could they leave Freedom for? For unfreedom? Admit it, that's just stupid!

26.

Eeney-Meeney-Miney-Moe

The friends and activists Khodzha Z and Danila L are walking through their very own consumer goods workshop at the end of the workday. The workday lasted twelve hours today. It was all hands on deck. Khodzha Z and Danila L see pretty girls and young men. Everything's gonna be fucked soon, says Danila L. Khodzha Z nods grimly. Their consumer goods shop is the only one that can save Freedom. After all, in a market economy you have to make more than guns. (Khodzha Z is taking evening classes, feverishly scraping together a degree in economics). It takes butter, too, all kinds of butter, such as: radio sets, electric meat grinders, specialized tools for cleaning sewer pipes (invented by our very own EDB), book-sewing machines, bows and arrows for preschoolers, kaleidoscopes, phonendoscopes, on-shore and shipboard radar systems, and, of course, the cancer-killing Golden Globe. We're the only ones who can actually do something, says Danila L, his trained eye noting how auntie Tanya, philologist and goods distributor—not to mention labor union rep and garment-industry liason—was slipping out the door with an armful of something mostly yellow, with flashes of color. Let's go have us a look.

The door to the office of auntie Panya Sikoyed, the Party organizer, is wide open. Outside the window reigns the February slush, the boundless and benevolent wet weather with its droplet-dotted twigs, its comfortable streetlamps, and its snow, brought to the boiling point of mercury and the burning point of alcohol. Party organizer Sikoyed is absent (in a meeting). Clusters of ladies' underthings foam and froth on her desk, the icing on an airy cake. There are enormous F-cup titslings, and brassieres a few sizes smaller, and saffron and caramel panties, and beige slips, and white slips, and even some black ones. Then from the next room the friends hear, but when will we get men's boots? When, when, *when*!? Last time they distributed them I didn't get any, and I'm a single mother, they have to give me men's boots first, before anybody else! They have to, they have to, they *have* to! We've got to tell the girls, says Z. Yes, we do, says L. They're having a hard time tearing themselves away from this avalanche of an image: under a red banner stands the Party organizer's desk, buried in masses of super-sensuous fabrics. Auntie Panya's sure gonna give Tanya an earful, once she sees her. That's okay, she's a philologist, she'll give as good as she gets.

The next day, L and Z proceed to Director V's office with their project: let's get selling! We have our Jazz, Rondo, and Camping transistor radios: the first is a deep, brilliant blue, the second is matte white, and the third is yellow with white trim. Why don't we set up a radio display in the Narva department store? Excellent! V lights up and beams. Great work! You're eagles! Can't lose with you around! I'll give you the prettiest girl in my office staff to be your saleslady! No, we don't need yours, we've got our own. Let us have Yelena E, urges Danila. She's got the best legs in the entire consumer goods shop. So be it, the director decrees. Done! And remember, advertising drives sales! Get the videocamera from J and make a few ads for local TV! L and Z are impressed and distressed by the director's enthusiasm. They get to work. Now they've turned their section of the Narva department store upside down, re-outfitted it. Z looks out the window and beckons to L: there's a streetlight right by the window! They promptly attach a remote antenna to the streetlight, paint the Earth onto the window, and attach a radio set decorated with extra lights at each of the four corners of the compass. The antenna's working. The radio receivers are receiving. The lights are flashing. Yelena E, the best legs in consumer goods (and all of Freedom), is smiling brighter than a star. Buyers mob the display. Eight hundred units are snapped up in three days: five hundred Jazzes, two hundred Rondos, and a hundred Campings. L and Z order silver brochures with navy-blue lettering from the Ministry of Foreign Trade.

"Chocolate!" shouts Director V. "We have to sell chocolate! Which of you knows how to make chocolate?!" The cafeteria is re-outfitted as a chocolate factory. Freedom's courtyard is lined with crackling March puddles. An intolerably chocolatey smell's suspended in the air. Special molds have been made in the prototype plant, while silver paper and red ribbon inscribed "Freedom Chocolate" have been ordered in quantity. A week later all the streets in the neighborhood, all the ditches and half-thawed streams, boast a gaudy coat of paper and ribbon; paper and ribbon have buried Ekaterinhof Park; and red ribbons float down the Ekaterinhof River, while wads of silver flash in the sun and rattle in the still-bare branches. Lev Ilych has got a good head on his shoulders, says L. Pepper! Put some pepper in it! shouts V, racing around the cafeteria and crashing into the cook-pots. Nobody in the USSR has ever made chocolate with pepper before, but I had it in America, it's very good!

And to top it all off, their ads finally appear on screens (text and screenplay by Z; produced by L and the Freedom Factory's entire consumer goods shop). The ad for the electric meat grinder is very simple. A vivacious, disheveled L appears onscreen (he looks for all the world like a student, you'd never guess he's twenty-nine and the father of a large family). What do you think, dear viewers, can the Freedom meat grinder grind up this tennis ball, or not? Let's find out! Drrr-t-zzzzz! It ground it right up. And here we have five burned-out light bulbs. Do you think it can handle them? D-drr-tzz-zz! It sure can! But what about this old issue of our dear weekly paper, *Glory to the Communist Party of the Soviet Union*, heh, heh! Attention! We are going to risk it! After all, it might break our instrument, oh dear... DN-DNRRRR-DRRTT-TT-TZZZZ-ZZZZ... shredded it! Sliced it to bits! Turned it into spaghetti! Pulverized it! Now there you have it, folks! And that'll happen to anything that touches our Freedom meat grinder! Whatever you do, just don't stick your diamonds in there! This last phrase was quickly snatched up by the public and put to frequent use, as was the Freedom meat grinder itself. Z's response to it all was, Lev Ilych has a good head on his shoulders! But he said it with a strange kind of look in his eye. Everything was in full swing, everything was fizzing along, the goods were in demand and selling well. Still, something was wrong.

Something's wrong, L repeated to himself as he walked down Volynkina Street. At the Narva department store on the corner of Strike Prospect, he spotted O, the chief economist, in the crowd. He was wearing a coat with the collar up and a half-empty rucksack hung on his back. Although L was still a ways off, he could sense that O's pose, O's very figure, conveyed extreme tension, even alarm. O was hawking kaleidoscopes. Business was brisk. Something's wrong, L said out loud. As he did, he happened to glance down. He flinched and stopped dead right where he was. A thick white line had been drawn with chalk all across Volynkina, across both crumbling sidewalks as well as the street. Underneath the line, right at L's feet, whoever drew the line had written "Eeny, meeny, miney, moe" in crooked letters. L spat out a curse and walked on, crossing the line.

27.

Fintensification

The Intensification-1991 Program shall ensure a significant how-much-of-this-can-we-take increase in fefectivity by replacing technical equipment and updating active enterprises, by maximlieing our current manuzotturing and R&D potential, by limfuhmenting across-the-board fauxtomation and limproved fequenfing, and by the broad application of cragressive I haven't been able to stand the sight of them since technological processes.

Fuck's *sake* these pointless meetings drive me nuts! With the overall aim fug reducing the workload on our mrrinting cushines, in the pock calendar year the top naghtaag crupducts and comhanents with the maximum hassible applicutions were defibouded and thnar crupduction method was vapidly switched to pressure cocking, which allowed us to reduce the amount fug ladud required to manuzotture comhanents by seventaag pizcent, to crupvisionally free up naght mrrinting cushines, and to efickomliee by saving more than twelve tons fug D16, the base mouderial. Taking finto ficksideration the imhartance and fibificance fug the government's cruphased it should be around here somewhere crupgram, our thousands-strong zottory collective has rineloped, and is broadly limfuhmenting, a multifuh-stage Fintensification crupgram, which wrrint unfold over the upcoming five-year pizdis. It was around here somewhere, I just can't remember where.

Everything's just hunky-dory, folks! Rineloping a mechanlieed crupduction capacity wrrint reshizauire an insbrtyl in the shizauantity fug CNC worshitaytions and the limfuhgidgation fug high-capacity cushines and speciomlieed worshitaytions that we nather buy or ke ourselves here at the zottory. One fug these high-capacity cushines with CNC is a multifuh-applicution vulste, an entire tooling center with a 24-instrugidg gazine Estanislao Carrera where's the money going to go? It switches instrugidgs fauxtoticomly, which naturomly omlows the opizator to insbrtyl the roude fug crupduction. Join us, brothers, if you think you've got what it takes to keep up! The line of sustaistr grinding cushines we have in our fauxtotion and revolverution shop omlowed us to insbrtyl the zone fug multifuh-cushine services and desbrtyl the number fug x-axis grinding CNC worshitaytions the zottory has had to acshizauire, the penditure fug technicom opizations on one vulste is not inficksiderable. Phew, these gullible types aren't long for this world.

Another amfh fug a crupcess enjoying nsbrtyld dend among the zottory collective is the successfully instomld mechanlieed vlste. The ficktinued insbrtyl in both sophisticution and shintity fug these vulstes wrrint greatly assist in the task fug yeblott apcrupdfgh dickit the comhnnts crupduced by the fauxtotion and mechanlieation departgidg fug the zottory itself, and limfuhgidged in a speciom worksho servicced by two skrrinted opizators. Bawk brawk ba-gawk the zottory fin two to two-and-a-homf tears to rinelop and put finto ss crupduction thirty types fug fauxtomouded and semi-fauxtomouded crupducts fug domooostic light industry and ficksumer goods ob bub key relevance ib tyw sectorzh, drbyl dyrdl trm tyr drr. The faxtomolded cnt semi-flertikned instrugidgs aborted he rex hd natidunom ando maystic usst meet and exceed the demanding dongstrds fu kniduction and bu do nof goods for hapular ass!

In short, comrades, Fintensification-1991 begins now! Ewe ah well-cam!

28.

Director NN. Intermedio.

Take a good look at this, we ain't never had nothin' like this before: from now on we're gonna *elect* our director! And seein' as how we're electing people now, then if we're electing somebody, it sure as pie ain't gonna be our dear Lev Ilych. No, sir. As long as we're having elections, then we'll elect... we'll elect whoever we want, that's who! But just as long as he's ideal. And we even know just who that is. You folks over in the Experimental Design Bureau, you got you your Director NN. People say he only sleeps four hours a night... You people are something else, snigger the engineers. We're not letting you take our NN. Because he's a genius, see. People write dissertations about his ideas. Stacks of 'em. But you want to grind him down on this coarse factory of yours. No way, yell the factory workers. Don't want to hear all that. We just want NN! At this point, the EDB gets good and truly worked up. Guys, guys, but you don't know him, see? He's not what you want! He's fragile. High-strung. Subtle. He's not a production worker, never has been, he doesn't know it. F's your man, elect him. No way, yell the factory workers. We want NN. We need NN. And that's final! Verka B is touched, she's actually not yelling, she's absently twiddling the corner of her kerchief in her fingers: your NN, see, he won't never shout… he's from the intelligentsia… we never had no directors like that before…

And here it is, election day. There are two candidates: V, the current director of the factory, and NN, the director of the EDB. Director V is certain he'll win. There's a spot of red on each cheek. He's lively, animated. He'd called Moscow the night before to speak to NN, who was there on a three-day business trip, and they'd had a friendly chat. They're not going to elect me, NN confirmed without regret. Of course not, V agreed. Factory's no place for you! V hung up, contented.

But things turned out differently.

Who is V, anyway? He's a tyrant, and a risk-taker, and thinks he's better than us! (Certain workers sigh.) He's been ruling over us since the Stagnation, remember all his cockamamie ideas? How much nonsense we had to deal with because of him?! Don't you remember his big idea about us making a microsynchrotron? And what about us, can't we do something?! Or is winning comedy competitions all we can do?! We elected our very own president, the kind of president we wanted! We didn't let the country go back to communism! But now are we really going to let our own dear enterprise get stuck with a buffoon who wants to keep everything the way it was?! What do you think he's going to do with it now there's such a thing as private property?! He's going to go back to paying us in trout, that's what! He has no conscience! But NN is a man of science! He's progressive! Take a look at his EDB: everyone in it's got a degree. And just take a look at his face! Could a man with a face like that ever deceive anybody? Or do things just for show? But Director V lied his whole life, he said he was a Communist but he hung around the church whenever he could! And now he'll hang around the church, but still keep his Party membership card tucked in his pocket! We're electing NN, gentlemen! And they did.

But NN was completely spent after his trip to Moscow. For three days he'd been twisting arms to get materials and components for prototype production, and then first thing he finds out when he gets back is he's been elected director of the factory. There he is, sitting in his office, head bowed, and he goes, no, I can't refuse. If the people want me, how can I not justify their trust? The only people with him are Tanechka and Chief Economist O. They're trying to talk him out of it: don't go, Your Grace, you'll perish. Yours is a different path. You're not cut out for the factory. You're fragile. High-strung. But production work is hard as iron. Running the EDB is one thing, but running a factory is another thing entirely. Just look at yourself, says Tanechka, crying. You need a vacation, not this. NN lifts his head. Thank you, Tanechka. But if they elected me, I've got to go. That's your masculine ambition talking! bursts out Chief Economist O. What ambition, scoffs, NN, waving the idea aside. With my blood pressure, I'm going to go belly-up here anyway. But that's what I mean! cries Tanechka hotly, fussing with hot water and lemon. Drink this! No, don't drink that! Wait! NN pushes the mug away and walks out of the office. No. We're not going to talk him out of it, says O. It's his fate. But what's going to happen to the factory? asks Tanechka. O shrugs. What do you think? Our factory's going to fall apart. It will be auctioned, privatized, the bandits will divide it up amongst themselves. Leave, Tanechka, and go work for the Social Insurance Fund. Labor union reps are welcome there. Tanechka shakes her head and swallows her tears. No. I'm not leaving the factory. If we're going under, let's go under together.

The Narva Outpost slides slowly into a horrific autumn evening in ninety-one. Only a few scattered windows light up.

The rusted-out beer stand, once called the Three Streams, went dry long ago. The cut ends of the copper cable from the BITC Dispatch System poke out of a nine-story building. A smashed telephone booth lies across Volynkina Street. The odor of vegetable rot emanates from basements. The park is as yet untouched, but here and there a few yellow spots have already appeared in the foliage. The moon, reflected in the muddy, foamy Ekaterinhof River, rises over the Central Tower; and it rises along the tram tracks; and V trails along the bank of the Ekaterinhof River, along the pallid, festering autumn grass, the bitter September grass, V, who the whole factory had just seen off at a good old-fashioned farewell party, who had genuinely been in peak form the whole time, bantering and exchanging kisses with everyone. Director V steps around the slippery trunk of an aspen, ripped roots and all out of the ground, he gets caught in its branches and stumbles, but grabs the trunk to steady himself. Director V doesn't fall down, rather, he stops, as always, just in time, right where the black, soft water stands silent. He sits down without looking, and again, he doesn't fall in; soft, dry willow branches catch him, gently bouncing up and down, they envelop him, entwine him. But V can't sit still, he stands up and takes a step forward, into the water, that is, into the thick, sticky sludge, sinking in up to the knee, and then another step, but then something grasps him forcefully from behind and brings him back to dry land. The warm evening lingers on, it feels as though that long, even warmth is the moon's. Lev Ilych, I'd bet my eyeteeth the factory's going to be needing you again, and pretty badly, too. V, bitter and regretful: should've nominated you, F. They'd've elected you. Listen to him! Now what kind of director would I be? All I know is my nuts and bolts. They're just idiots. You stick around another dozen years or so. No, no, V demurs passionately, his small hand waving away dissent. This is it for me! Come on, you know it's not. It'll be hard, that's true. But it's going to be hard for everybody now. Here, let's call your driver. But what about you? I'm headed back to the factory. You're crazy. It's already night. Yeah, but I have something I've got to finish there. (They are standing in the middle of the asphalted intersection. V's trousers dry quickly in the light of the hot, dry moon. His boots are still quite wet.) Hey, listen. Go easy on NN. He's not the factory type. Why is he sticking his neck out? They'll eat him alive, I swear to God they will. There'll be some tough times ahead. Pshaw, tough times. In Freedom there was never any other kind.

29.

Thread Your Own Noses

Tanechka, the philological labor union rep, sits in her office. The door is wide open. She gets almost a hundred sets of workplace leaving papers a day. That means twelve an hour. One set every five minutes. Every five minutes, one person quits his job at the Freedom Factory. That's two thousand people gone a month. Two thousand people a month quit their jobs at the Freedom Factory. And this isn't the first month of this. The factory is melting away. Soon there'll be nothing left of it.

Tanechka sees herself in two mirrors. She looks at her profile out of the corner of her eye. She's pretty. Maybe her profile's just the tiniest bit softer around the edges. She's young. Her head's no longer crowned with a tower. Tanechka razed it and produced (erected) a hairdo of gray and reddish feathers.

Each morning, a dwindling rivulet creeps down Volynkina Street. Its traces are fading. The pondside park's vacant. The factory courtyard's a blank space. Tanechka smokes by the window. The sharp freezing air isn't allowing the smoke out. So that's the end of the Experimental Design Bureau. All the engineers abandoned ship, leaving behind just ten workers and a Kuhlmann drafting machine.

Back in those first days of the exodus, Tanechka was still trying to do something. There she is, standing in a half-empty workshop, trying to convince gaunt, glum Tolik to wait until the end of the month. But Tolik's wife also works at Freedom, and this is the fifth month the factory hasn't paid them, and they have two kids at home. Tolik listens to her as he chews a bite of bread and drinks water with five-minute blackcurrant jam. In the summer they put up jars and jars of it from their plantations. Now they stir in a teaspoonful per glass and get a salutary, sweetish swill. This is all Tolik can count on today. But tomorrow? Tanechka stops trying to convince him.

And that's the end of Workshop Six... there go Twelve and Sixteen... There are still a few left in Nineteen. All of Four quit the same week. It ripped itself out by the roots. There were lots of young people in it; what are young people going to do here? The only ones left are old folks, the ones who have nowhere else to go. The rest have filtered away, out into the derelict tracts where towering slabs of salt-encrusted, stony snow are stacked on the shoulder of the road, where a murky sun hangs above endless rows of stalls and mechanics' shops. Nobody needs us, said Chief Economist O to Tanechka; he kissed her goodbye and died.

Gradually Tanechka begins to sense that she doesn't really feel like talking anymore, or working, or doing anything at all. Strange thoughts come into her head. What has she spent her life on? On this factory here. What factory? There is no factory anymore. Who is she? No family. No accomplishments. What can a labor union be now? Nothing. But every day she fights with the new chief financial officer, arguing that the factory has to issue the standard milk ration for harmful work conditions to the women in the galvanizing shop, at no cost to them, no matter how many of them there are. And every day, while she's signing leaving papers, she still tries to—not change their minds, no, but just to say something, to mention something in parting, something they'll remember, so that later, someday, maybe they'll want to come back.

Once, late in the day, who comes knocking at her door but Danila L, a young guy of around thirty who used to work in the consumer goods shop, but now is some kind of gopher, F's deputy Director of operations, something like that, but what difference does it make now, who's what. Ah, your turn. Well, let's have your papers, then. And I did used to wonder what such a promising guy was doing out there in... Danila shakes his head. Oh, no, I'm not leaving, what makes you think that? Just the opposite. I wanted to ask you something. I don't know, maybe it's stupid... Have a movie night at the factory. For everyone who's stayed. 'Cause we do have movies about the factory, back from Director N's days. From Director V's days, too. Let's draw up a poster, get folks together in the auditorium, and show these movies. At least it'll be some kind of... non-material stimulus. Yeah. What do you say? It can't make things worse, anyway... I'd kind of like to watch the one about the comedy troupe, see how me and Z used to get the crowd going... And you'd be interested in seeing the ones about the collective farms, the hay and straw, the Golden Globe... Let's do it, Tanechka agrees, astounded.

It's dark and cold in the auditorium. People are wearing their overcoats and jackets. Forty or fifty have come, the rest are hurrying home after work or kicking around the city trying to scare up some cash. It's mainly old folks watching. The Freedom Factory. Here it was, in the difficult year of 1928, that a brigade of young shockworkers was formed for the very first time, the precursor of our communist labor brigades. Today, this is one of our foremost industrial enterprises. The external appearance of the original building is the only thing left from the old days. The factory has grown up and grown young again before the very eyes of our veterans of labor and war. Their work has done much to ensure that young people can labor in newly rebuilt and remodeled workshops and laboratories, where we have created the ideal conditions for productive labor, for the expression of individual initiative in labor. Every year the factory replenishes the working class anew with graduates of schools, vocational schools, and technical institutes. (F, cigarette in hand, surreptitiously appears in the doorway. He doesn't look at the screen. He blows the smoke out the door.) The Aster, a device made in our factory, is required for the safe navigation of large seafaring vessels in low-visibility conditions. The high precision of these units, and their reliability when far out at sea, are the fundamental requirements of our principal client, the Ministry of the Maritime Fleet of the USSR. (Odious officialese. Party clichés. Dusty banners. Back then, nobody could care less about these films. Now these few sit watching them, and they want to leave, but they can't stop watching.) After that, the athletic battles moved out to the watery mirror of the lake. The lakeshore was transformed into something like bleachers for the fans, whose cries and exhortations carried out to the competitors, giving them strength to compete for their team's victory. The team from Nikolay Gusev's shop bay has emerged victorious in this resolute athletic struggle. And finally, the solemn moment has arrived when the teams are to be honored and the games are to be ended, games in which more than 120 people, or one fifth of the entire Shop collective, have participated. Someone sniffles quietly into a hanky.

Two mighty fabricators from shop Nine, K and K, get up quietly (they were sitting at the end of a row) and noiselessly head out the door. There they are met by F's open-armed embrace. Well, K and K, it's you, F whispers grimly. I heard you'd gotten it in your heads to leave. But the pay's bad, plead the fabricators. There's no orders. No orders?! F advances on them, a baleful, blue-gray stormcloud. But who's going to mint the metro tokens? And who's going to rivet together the advertising columns? And what about the crematorium fence?! You want to try telling me that's not an order?! You've both gone out of your friggin' minds!! You will stay at the factory!! You'll thread your own noses if you have to, but you're not leaving! Because without you, there is no factory!! You got that!?

30.
DOA

Good lord, what a mess. Here we were thinking they're regular renters, making fur coats out of stray cats and whatnot. But turns out they'd started manufacturing knock-off high-end vodka on Freedom's grounds. All the other renters will have to be checked too, you hear, Inga? The director has no idea, the director's very ill. Thank our lucky stars he's still drawing breath at all. We have to protect him. But all we got is us: you plus me makes we. What? What shouldn't the chief engineer have to do? The chief engineer of a factory has to do everything. And the lawyer also has to do everything. Yes, down to finding the fire safety bucket. And dumping the cigarette butts out of it, yes, that's exactly right. Although, actually, our chief engineer's usually the one who dumps the butts. So anyway, you go on and check all the renters. You head left, I'll head right. We'll go through our entire secret manufacturing facility and audit everyone who rents from us. Training courses for killers? Fabulous. Rat-meat pies? Sure, a fine business. Whore auditions? Welcome. Printing counterfeit documents? Make yourself at home. Accounting? You collect on accounts receivable? Hmm... nope, we'll have to part ways. Basically, Inga... Inga! I just thought of this! People could embed spies here. Can't you just see it? A spy comes over and rents our snow melt pit. He pretends to be running a regular, quiet little dog shelter, but he uses the dogs' barking to broadcast coded messages out of the pit.

That's life, Inga! These days all of us at the factory have the same problem: DOA. No, it's not that, and not the division of administration, either. It's that we've got to do over and above. Take me, the chief engineer. Before me it was the legendary H. He could take one look at a device and repair its defects with his unaided gaze alone. I could maybe do the same thing, sure I could! But the problem is that there are no devices anymore, there's nothing left but defects! There's nothing to look *at*!

Or take you, Inga. The lawyer. Before you, it was also Inga, the legendary Inga I. You look a lot like her. Like her when she was young. Just as pretty, thin, and smart. Inga had a harder job than you: she had to observe unjust laws as she fought for justice. But your job is to make justice profitable for us. Our subcontractor's factory was shut down, its director ruined, its equipment sold for scrap, and it's all Freedom's fault. Or take that City Water and Sewer Services! Oh, City Water, you devil! You and your announcement filling the bottom of the entire first page of the *Petersburg Workdays*, you and your announcement titled "They Make Our Lives Harder," with its boldface lists of all the enterprises that haven't paid their city electric or water bill! We can't seem to clamber our way up out of that announcement. What's this eminent entity, this kindly City Water, saying? It's saying, I'm not going to let Freedom so much as pour a cup of tea, not to mention pour its wastewater out the drainage canal. I'm going to make them all cry, it says. Inga, don't you find it funny? It wants to make us cry, you and me. Or F. It wants to make F cry. It might as well make the Narva Gate cry. But why is City Water so unfeeling, Inga? How can City Water, that red-eyed devil, be so sure that everything in its own life will always be hunky-dory? Or maybe it's just the opposite, it's desperate? What do you think?

Now me, I figure I don't have any right holding back the workers' pay for yet another month. They'd like to have themselves a little something to eat. City Water has plenty to eat. And it'll wait. If it arranges to shut off the water, we'll do like we did last time. You remember how it was last time, Inga? Oh, yes, that was before you. We just went and unscrewed the valve and posted a guard with a rifle next to it. That's against the law, you say. Well, we didn't have a lawyer back then. I'm confident you'll be able to come up with something better. That's not sarcasm! That's faith in you as a specialist. Let's go, Inga. I need a list of our renters by sundown.

So, here we are. What'd you find? Hold on a minute, Mikhail Stepanovich, I found something a lot better. (They are walking over to the infamous snow melt pit.) Help me jump down. Inga, you'll kill yourself down there. Why are you… what do you want down there? I have an uneasy premonition that you shouldn't be down there. Help me, I said! Our salvation from that announcement and from City Water is down there! Thank you. And now, please get me that little yellow trowel. It should be under that bush, just a little dirt sprinkled on it to hide it. Inga, I'm intrigued. What can all this possibly mean from a legal standpoint? This is what it means. Jump down here to me. Plop!

Look here, Mikhail Stepanovich. Okay. I'm looking. Well now, and what have we here? It's a frame. The frame of a really old well. If that pit of yours hadn't collapsed and had to be repaired, it'd still be hidden. Do you understand what this means? It means that we have our own autonomous source of water, on factory grounds. What we have here is access to an

underground freshwater lens. Wow, Inga! Now that's a law degree for you! Admit it, they teach you all to dowse in law school, don't they? How on earth did you come up with this? I looked at an old map in the factory archive. Nobody'd ever paid any attention to it before. No time. Or just nobody needed to. Inga! Why don't you go ahead and find oil and gas on Freedom's grounds, too, and then we'll apply to Strasbourg for the status of independent state. Why not? We'll take care of our own weapons, oil and gas. For the rest we'll depend on our renters. But that City Water, now! Oooh, yes, City Water! Ho-ho! We'll give that red-eyed devil a shiner! Go ahead, turn our water off! Ha-ha, Inga, you're a genius! Let's have us a little victory dance, ma'am!

What in the world are you doing, esteemed colleagues? We're having a production meeting. In the pit? It's not a pit. It's a mountain! Um, Mikhail Stepanovich, I also wanted to tell you what kind of renters I found. One of them's the Senegalese Embassy. It wouldn't be a big deal, except that they have their leader's magic mirror hanging in there and you can go through it to Senegal, and also to some kind of world of white bones, I don't know what all... Don't give a damn, Inga! We pasted City Water a good one. Well, the second unpleasant discovery is the high-volume production of an unknown white powder. I strongly suspect it to be heroin. There's a couple of sacks in there, about forty kilos apiece. Heroin. That's bad. Get some alcohol from F and set fire to it on the sly. Just don't set the building on fire, or else you'll be the one who has to weasel out of the fines after. We pasted City Water a good one! Bravo, Inga! As soon as we get some more orders in, I'll give you a bonus. Let's go have some tea.

31.

Before Dawn

Director NN wakes up, falls back asleep, and wakes back up
again. His agonized drowsing goes on and on, refusing to resolve itself in either sleep or wakefulness. He can't feel his
body in his sleep, but he can see it before him, like a map of a
forest, like a bearskin, like a taxidermied or field-dressed car-
cass of the country, its cankers and holes glowing in the dark.
He falls asleep, wakes up, and falls asleep, or maybe he's coming to life, dying, and coming back to life again. A lake in the
forest, or rather a swamp, gleams before Director NN's eyes:
water deep in fissures smacks its lips. Grass is springy, green,
and disgusting. He can smell wild mint, aspen, and labrador
tea, and a loud cluster of poison-yellow birds clatters in some
branches. They're talking with NN: sign it, sign it, or we'll
crush you.

But NN can't sign it, so moss smothers his face and chest,
something's gurgling and seething, clumps of moss rip pain-
fully out of their beds, exposing horrible sores where the earth
was rubbed raw, but it's skin, not earth, half-decomposed skin
covered in scars, or it's the corpse of the country, or it's his
very own hand, just with holes pierced through it at random,
the holes brimming with a reeking, combustible slurry. Petro-
leum. Sign it, NN, sign it, or we'll crush you.

NN wakes up, yanks himself out of his dream, and sits on the edge of the bed. For a while he just sits, a heavy piece of condensed murk in the thin dark of the room, faintly lit from outside. With enormous effort, he stands. His heartbeats are rapid and nauseating. Need to open the window and get a drink of water. Can't take this. NN literally falls onto a chair in the kitchen. They'll kill me. Hell with them. They're killing everybody. But I'm not gonna do it. Then after you're gone D the Odessan will do it for you, or else F, the operations director, will do it, or that optimistic deputy director of his, Danila L. They could intimidate Inga. They could just take the factory by brute force. Nothing to it: just take a defense industry factory by force. This kind of thing is going on everywhere you look. It happens every day. Throwing your life away won't change anything. His mouth goes dry again, but he can't take any more water. Bitter, prevernal freshness pours in through the ventilation window. NN says again, clearly and distinctly: I will not divide Freedom up into shares. Fine, but haven't all the Ninth Directorate's enterprises already been auctioned off? They have. And blood was spilled for every single one of them. Would it really be better to let the state keep Freedom? Did we hear that right: the state? The thing that's absolutely no different from us crooks? They're the exact same crooks, buddy. Didn't you know that your whole life you've been working for crooks? Maybe you're a communist, eh, NN, like that shop foreman of yours, Pavel Pavlich P, who keeps his party membership card close to his heart to this very day? You want to go on kissing their asses, just to get the same thing you're already getting now: zero orders to fill? How many months have your workers been going hungry? Veterans of labor who drudged night and day for fifty years for the state! They were betrayed. And you've been betrayed.

That's all true. They haven't eaten in six months. The state lies to us and betrays us. But there's not going to be any deal. And this isn't the state not letting Freedom go. This is Freedom giving the state credit. Freedom's not taking anything, buddy, it's giving it. Long-term and interest-free. We are prepared to wait and work as long as it takes. We'll wait another half century, if we need to. We'll wait another half millennium. We have D the mechanic. We have Tasya the finisher. We have D from Odessa. And we have Director NN, formerly a brilliant scientist, who got sucked into this meat grinder against his own volition, who constantly makes mistakes, who's weak, not hard enough on people, can't see things through, who fobs important decisions off on his subordinates. All true. But you'll sell our Freedom off over my dead body.

32.

Director L. Intermedio.

parallel, a parallel production structure, churly-wurly-chur, emphasis on production-line assembly, but a ponytail like a raven's wing, or smoke and smiles over the softest, most sunken-in sofa, and everything here's going, going, going, restructuring, re-reproduction, reduction, there's no reason, there's no reason to fight, to find out, they're going in one by one, they roll back inside, they crowd their way in, all the familiar smells, now bring out all the loose ends, drag them out into the open, all the ones that were mentioned over the course of the past five hours – could somebody please open a window?

inhales deeply the state has abandoned us, the worst part is that our sales have just completely stopped, you understand, everybody but me, but I stayed, everything can't keep just going downhill forever, structural transformation, the current demand for goods, India, China, whatever you like, we were able to get back on course, the remnants of defense industry orders, there is work, they've got the fire in the belly again, even if it is just for a little while, the workers got paid, seems like an uptick, even if it is just a small one, but that was our doing, thanks to us the factory will get ahold of itself get back up on its feet dust itself off make a name for itself in the market strengthen its employee base commence structural transformations

to cut them off, but we have to scale back unprofitable units, liquidate them, structural transformation of production, to get working, making not meat grinders but what our factory knows how to make, what it should make, F and I created it, we transformed it, we had to reduce our square footage many times, endless optimizations, F became director of operations, I was his deputy, D ran around plugging up holes and saved the factory from ruin, we set up a new parallel production structure, but NN was all no, it's too hard, too much conjecture, churly-wurly-chur, always the same answer no matter

I do everything, everything, but it all just disappears, sinks down a well, sinks into deep muck, we made the proposal, but they are hanging around our necks, holding us back, we don't need them anymore, I only have one, there's nobody else who can, I have to leave first of March, in seven weeks, they escorted him out, under the pretext of personnel reduction, I was out drumming up orders, it all rests on me, all the marketing, the entire database, but they couldn't care less, they'll cut us off and not blink an eye, they're not the factory, F and me, we're the factory

his enormous accomplishment, and nobody's trying to say otherwise, his only accomplishment was that he did not allow it to be divided up and auctioned off, but he just barged on ahead, without seeing where the road led, because those people, you know, he's not a production worker, he's a scientist, and to make matters worse he'd gone almost totally blind, people turned cruel a result of those years, what courage and strength of spirit you had to have, and NN did have it, to stand against those predators, those creditors, no matter what, we could build a monument to him, but you understand, right, that he had no idea how a factory should be run, how it should develop, our proposals just spun their wheels, got no traction, but his people were everywhere, and that mindset was everywhere, it was a downright horror show, he dragged people from one shop to another, he dragged people in, every Tom, Dick, and Harry came running, it was insane, the overhead expenses, and how are F and me supposed to deal with this, the factory was spinning its wheels, just spinning its wheels, it was hemorrhaging people, and the whole time we tried and tried to do something, but they kept putting the brakes on us and then the good life in quotation marks started up again

do you see what's happening F and me concentrated everything on production, we devoted ourselves to evening out the imbalances in production we increased the workload for shops that weren't operating at full capacity I personally went around getting orders making calls to all the enterprises that was when we started making waveguides for example several shops got work right away finally we got everybody working at full capacity and those extra orders were no longer necessary, but then it happened again, and again, everything is cyclical, after all, but we hadn't had time to build up some fat, we'd only just barely had time to catch our breath a little, and then again comes an idle period, and sitting idle for a factory is a very difficult business you still have to pay the workers' salary the whole time and then they didn't pay for three months at a time, again, and it was let's reduce personnel, again

what I want, what I want is for either F or me (don't worry) I don't care, what I want is for the factory to, to churly-wur-ly-chur, it's my nature, I want to stick with a smokestack, so that – this is the first place I ever worked, you know, there's exactly one entry in my work record, but they're going to fire me, in two months I have to clear out of the – I'm not afraid of it, I'll leave, of course, that's not the point – but who are you? – who are you? – tell me, just give me a clue, who sent you? – is there anything you can do? – I understand, I understand what you're doing, go ahead and keep on keeping mum, I understand everything, you're young, you're living it up, you tell me what you need, that's the main thing, because I have to save the factory, F and me won't let anything else

I do have faith in a bright future, it has nothing to do with you, or with the president, or with the country's entire military complex, I just have faith, let them fire me, I'm not going to go drown myself in the Ekaterinhof River, I just want to save the factory, I want to save Tatyana S and my F, I want to save everything here, and get a new order to produce the Golden Globe, I want a lot of things, your country can go fuck off, and your president too, so help me, I don't give a shit about defense readiness, or your cigars, or your these are gray days, it hurts me more than you, but I will do everything you ask, because what you've done has got my back to the wall, it already had Director V's back to the wall, this democracy of yours, this dictatorship, I don't give a shit what it's called, I don't fucking care, I just want the women in the galvanizing shop to get their milk every day, if you do that I'll do everything for you, if you do that I'll save you, but if you can't do that, then you can fuck the hell off

---

I can't say anything else no I can't say whether he was mixed up in this I can't say anything about it

reduced, hounded, and useless to everybody here except F, I came to a meeting one morning, and early in the morning the silence was shattered by a phone call from Moscow today you have a new acting director his last name is L and I went in and it was a shock nobody knew about it only a select few knew and I said as of today we are going to start working differently and we started working differently and that summer I passed a competitive selection and I was named director of the Freedom Factory (and I don't give a shit what they meant and I'm not going to pay them in any way we already paid dearly and in full and now we're going to work and move forward we're going to work and we don't owe them anything else)

33.
Goblins

They call us goblins. And why? Well this is why: because that's what we are. Plain and simple. That's the way we started out, and that's the way we ended up. It's no big deal, just don't be scared of us, that's all. I came to the factory in 1984 doing the same thing I do now: operating CNC milling machines. And right away I started playing soccer. Our factory team was the Asters. They made me captain right away. I think that if I'd played, I'da gone pro. But I ended up a milling machine operator. I love my job. That's important, loving your job. Now don't you go being afraid of me! What are you afraid of me for? Natasha! Natakha, sweetie, don't nobody need to be afraid of me, right? See, Natakha says you don't!

I live over the drugstore. Our communal apartment was broken up in the nineties, but I wouldn't budge: I'm not moving, and you can't do a damn thing about it. I'm not moving, not even to a four-bedroom. I'm not moving anywhere. So they left me there, me and my family. And they wanted to shove me way out into BFE, onto Science Prospect! Like I need that: Science friggin' Prospect! I'm right here, I've got all the stores, the Neva, every day I get to work on my own two feet, just hustle over the bridges. Petersburg's basically my hometown. And I love playing soccer more than anything in the world. And my job, too. And that's all there is to it.

In the nineties it kind of slacked off, but in the oughts it picked back up again. In 2006 we put together a team, I was named captain, and we won the factory championship right off the bat! It is true that we slid a little this year, we came in third. But we still place every year. We place every single year. What? We're working up a women's team too, right, Natakha? Oh, yeah! Natakha'll fill you in. We have practice on Thursdays and Fridays. We rent a whole indoor field specially for that. At first I thought nobody'd show up. But show up they did! It's not just old fogeys at the factory anymore! And nobody skips practice! They've got the fire, we're keeping it going!

And the reason they call us goblins... well it makes perfect sense, since whenever we get on the bus... it's basically just like, when we're getting on the bus, to go to a big camping meet, we—so what?! It means our team's the only one where the players do whatever the captain says, the minute he says it! The minute I say it, that is. 'Cause I'm always captain. Who else?! When I say jump, it's "how high?" I know just who to have walk on his hands, or who climbs ropes best. Listen to what happened to us once. Three guys went out in a boat. They went out there, basically somewhere out there in the Gulf. And then it was time for us to leave. The Coast Guard rescue boat heads out to see what's up. It gets there and they're all like, we don't know, no idea, three people headed out, but now there's only two in the boat. I broke out in a cold sweat. What'd they do with the third one? Turns out they'd let him off on shore somewhere. He eventually got back on his own. What a fucking idiot! Boy, the things I've put up with!

So anyway, we're goblins because we run rings around everybody else. We always win. I'm usually team captain. The competitions are different every time, they never repeat one. We're already joking that it's time for us to star in a reality show. So this year, for example, when they told me it'd be horses, I thought, what the heck are we gonna do with them? Some of us can't even get up on a horse… but it turned out that only ten of us had to sit on them, and the other ten could just lead them by the bridle. Piece of cake, we figured it out, got on up there… some people even climbed up more than once. I rode all the way to Helsinki. Things are really cheap there, nothing but sales everywhere. The horse swam. Then we went back, had something to eat, and headed into the city. Ever since then that's all I've wanted, is to ride. Too bad there's nowhere to keep a horse. Can't just gas it up, either. Horse's too complicated.

Once there was a skittles competition, you know, where you throw the bat at the pins? We had no fewer than twenty-eight for that one! And I was the head referee. I had to look up the rules on the Internet. Star, arrow, machine gun… neat stuff. So we grabbed the bats and got down to it. One guy goes, I'm gonna throw it over the Central Tower. Set the pins up on the roof there for me. So our guys are like, no problem. They go up there and set them up. And this guy rears back and slings that bat as hard as he can, and crash! Right through F's window it goes. And there's a meeting going on in there, everybody's yelling at each other, and this guy's bat lands smack in the middle of his shop foreman's forehead, pow! Right when F was giving that foreman a real good chewing-out. Everybody kind of interpreted the bat as F being maybe a little too harsh, a little over the top. But F didn't blink an eye: he grabs the bat and pegs it right back, and he hits the guy right in the forehead, too. No big deal; he just had a scar there afterwards. It happens. Bat was more of a boomerang, heh.

And there was this other time, when some older guys came up to me and said, what about us, what sport can we compete in? We decided to have a domino tournament! Thirty-six players, the competition was intense. The players' average age was eighty-five. We had every kind of game you can imagine! One winter, we had a tug-of-war in the snow. The director was the referee. A whole crowd of fans came.

There was this one obstacle course, it was really a piece of work. It wasn't all that easy to get through. There was one condition: the course had to be completed six times, but it didn't matter which six people did it. The same person could do it all six times, if you wanted. So we entered five men and one woman. When one of the guys couldn't do it, our gal went through it a second time! Once for herself, and once for the guy. I was pleasantly horrified to know I had a person who could do *that* on my team. And yeah, you all call us goblins. Maybe we are goblins, but nobody else can do it! Maybe we don't exactly behave all, you know, proper and obedient, but the upside is that we're the only ones you can really count on! This one time, on our last big camping meet, one of our young ladies got lost. She went off into the bushes to pee and then came out the wrong direction, and just kept going. We combed through the entire forest and found her. There just happened to be a military unit there... they'd caught her and were holding her down, and... well, we got there just in time, basically. If we'd got there a minute later, then the meet... let's just say that the meet wouldn't've been a success. And you call us goblins! If we weren't goblins, we couldn've sent that unit packing! Right, Natakha? See? Listen to the lady!

Now if we could just get a billiards championship going... but all the tables have holes. We need to get new tables, even just two. Folks want tables. Tables without holes.

34.

The Call

Night draws on, black and windy like last night. The wind cries in the stovepipe and vents, it whines at all the windows. Everything's awash in the color black. Black offers the eye many shades. Brilliant black and transparent black, thick black and thin. Director L gets in bed and falls right to sleep. His wife is next to him. The phone rings. Director L knows who it is. He wakes right up and lifts the receiver. It's the designer of the Golden Globe. He had a stroke, so he can't talk, but he calls the director every night. This, too, falls within the scope of Danila L's responsibilities. Yes, says L. Hello.

X is silent. This is how he says what L must hear. It's entirely likely that he's discussing a new modification for the Golden Globe. Although no one can know for sure; maybe X is trying to say something else. At any rate, these daily phone calls are a very effective means. They show that X wants to get through to Director L. Through a wall of silence and incomprehension.

But L is a good kid, uncomplicated (used to be). He needs all these mystical flourishes like he needs a hole in the head. Of course, X doesn't need them either. It's just that everything in X's head went a little askew. Everything became brightly lit somehow, brightly colored. And so he calls, every night.

Perhaps it seems to him that it's all one and the same call. But for us and for L this single call breaks down, splits into many layers, one for every night. Every night. Who's right, nobody's right, everybody's right… ah, bite me.

Hello, yes, says L. I'm listening.

Silently X talks on and on, eloquently and with conviction. He says, but won't we lose the market? Look, we got down to work on the Golden Globe-M. "Modernized." Meaning, we got down to work as best we could. But the conditions! We need a new storage area. Right now they just sit outside after we assemble them! What we really need is to build a storage shed. And it'd also be good for us to buy a waterjet cutting machine, that could cut the sheet metal for the Globe cabinets using a mix of sand and water. It's ecologically safe, it doesn't give off harmful substances while it's cutting the metal. You could set it up next to a baby's cradle! And then there's a whole series of things I'd like to have… we need a welding shop, where rows of Golden Globes could hang in caravans, like caravans of camels… Overall we need a lot of things, so we don't fall behind Canada and the Czech Republic.

We're hoping to be approved for the government's procurement program, Ivan Borisovich, says L. Then you'll get both your waterjet cutter, and your…

In stony silence the minutes tick past and the orator's speech flows in torrents. The darkness on the street shifts its position. The golden darkness under the streetlamps. The muteness of winter without snow. The gray pavement. L sits with the phone pressed to his ear. He doesn't doze. This is one of the director's responsibilities. The last responsibility of the day and the first responsibility of the night.

Hello, yes, I'm here, says L.

But the night will hold another responsibility: to dream. Director N, in white belted vestments, will explain what to do with the factory, or the President of Russia, in radiant chambers, will watch L furiously making a case for why Khodorkovsky should be freed. All of L's dreams are furious, to the extent that upon waking he doesn't immediately make himself forsake the blankets; he rolls over a few times, gets up, and only begins living five minutes after his awakening.

No, you can't do it that way, says L, objecting to X's furious mute speech. I wouldn't lay it out so unconditionally.

On the other end something's happening, X's mood has changed, and L knows beyond a shadow of a doubt that now he'll get an earful, a lecture, an incensed tirade. He won't hear it, admittedly, but that doesn't make it any easier. The ear that's pressed to the phone starts burning. X's blather scatters silently all over the room. What could all that have been about, thinks L, but then he's not thinking at all anymore, since he's dropping the phone, while on the other end, X puts the phone back in its cradle, but now nobody will ever know what he's thinking while he does so (X has locked himself up and thrown away the key), and what L's thinking is—he's not thinking anything, he's sinking into sleep, drowsing in the golden gloom, illuminated from a streetlight outside, and his wife is next to him, and little by little L fades away, drifts off, eternity is passing over them, X isn't going to say anything else; the silent air has turned word-less. The snow starts up in earnest. By morning the streeets are lightly coated; by noon, they're thickly covered.

35.

One of Us

At one time Volynsky's dacha stood where our factory is now. Artemy Volynsky, he was one of those aristocrats back in Empress Anna Ivanovna's reign, heard of him? I looked him up. Volynsky was a cabinet minister—back in those days a man in the service couldn't hope to rise any higher than that—but then they executed him. Why? Who the heck knows? But it wasn't for any mythical conspiracy, which there wasn't, actually, and it definitely wasn't for petty little sins like taking five hundred rubles from the Department of Stables, that's ridiculous, because *all* high-ranking officials took money back then. And it goes without saying that he overdid it. He himself admitted that he had a difficult personality, that he was impetuous and hot-tempered, but that's not the point. It's just that by the time he got into the cabinet, a certain consensus had been reached in Russian politics, basically in the entire court; a kind of drowsy tranquility that satisfied everybody. Volynsky came along and started shaking things up, though all the things he did and proposed doing were routine administrative measures. Increasing productivity in certain areas, intensification, reasonable measures in the spirit of continuing what Peter the Great had begun. None of this had the slightest whiff of the revolutionary. It is true that he had other dreams, too. But it wasn't about the dreams. He certainly wasn't hiding them. He publicly announced all his projects, assuming, correctly, that there was nothing seditious in them. Because there wasn't anything seditious about them! It was just the fact that he did it. Volynsky disregarded the established consensus. He fell out with Osterman. He began reporting directly to the empress, without Osterman's mediation. And so we end up in the following situation: first Volynsky suggests some resolution, then Osterman writes an objection. As soon as Volynsky arrives at the cabinet, Osterman leaves, so as not to see him. And so on. Near the end Osterman flat-out stopped attending cabinet meetings and Volynsky was the only person who reported directly to the empress. So then Biron himself, Anna's favorite, starts to see Volynsky as a competitor, someone just as powerful and audacious as him.

There are things that are never documented. We will never know what Biron said to Anna. She sat on the fence for a long time. It took a long time to convince her that Volynsky had to be executed. The execution had a kind of performative, demonstrative cruelty, a certain sense of revenge, but it was more Biron's revenge than Anna's. To Anna, Volynsky was a loyal servant. (When she lay dying, she said her death was payback for Artemy.) Everyone knew he was no traitor. The sentence doesn't even mention the concept of treason. He was incriminated in a plot to get the officers of the Guard on his side and claim the throne himself, it was delusional, absolute nonsense. But all his confidants confessed under torture that he wanted to take the throne. It's not that anybody seriously thought he was actually capable of doing such a thing. But the very fact they decided to charge him with something like this says a lot: it means it was believable that on top of everything else, he'd want to try and take the throne, too. He himself categorically denied any such intent, in spite of the rack and other tortures.

They wanted to put him to death by impalement. Impalement is in a class by itself, you need to realize that it could be a matter of several days, since the person being impaled sinks down lower and lower onto the spike, gradually ripping himself apart from the inside, but the empress was merciful and commuted the sentence to being drawn and quartered. First he and his confidants' tongues were cut out, and their mouths were wrapped shut with rags that got completely soaked with blood, and after that they were led to the scaffold, where Volynsky's right hand was cut off, and then his head. And why? Why was he put to death? For the simple fact that at some point he became different.

At some point everything suddenly flips, and this difference becomes the main thing. You're horrified, suddenly, as you realize: I didn't live right, everything I ever did was wrong.

A lot of people think I came back because I got my business taken away from me. No. It's not like that. Or rather, my business really was taken away from me, but that was much earlier, and it wasn't the first business I've lost. I know how to lose things, I know how to get back up and start everything all over again, and I actually had started all over again, for the third time already. I opened up, again, it was really hard, but we'd begun to do okay again. By that time, the time I'm talking about, we'd almost managed to make it to the point where, well, not where you don't have to worry, but where the company is alive, where your work day moves along normally. That's what my situation was at that time. I'd been a businessman for twenty years, a whole lifetime, and at that particular time I wasn't bankrupt, I wasn't up a creek. It's just that our factory director called me, the same guy I worked side-by-side with back in the day, and he said, come back.

You might be thinking, in what way is this "our" factory, when the factory was always state-run? Whereas the business I had, for example, really was mine? Yeah, I don't know what to say to that. I don't have an answer explaining why it's this way, not that way. I asked, well, how long will you give me to think it over? He goes, five minutes. Yeah, I didn't even need that.

Why I was telling you about Volynsky? That's easy. Our factory's on his land, on the place where his dacha used to be. Well, no, I mean his ghost doesn't haunt our shops at night or anything, in this country we've been through so much that we'd have a whole mob of ghosts. Tortured girls from the Stieglitz textile factory and all that. But yes, it's on his land, that's why the street is named Volynkina. At one time I got interested in it and stumbled across this story, this person; I started to get down into the details, it really hooked me, and then I unexpectedly came across his portrait in this book, here, I'll show it to you, and you'll understand why I'm so, you know, into these things

amazing? I find this so amazing

(The night before he was executed, Volynsky had a dream. He is entering an unfamiliar, completely dark church. A priest approaches him. The priest's face and clothing are visible, in spite of the darkness. Volynsky asks why the candles aren't being lit. "Wait," the priest replies. "You'll see, they'll all burn." Volynsky recounted his dream to the officer guarding him, one Kakovinsky, and they were both amazed when the priest Fyodor Listiyev came into the cell to shrive the criminal before the execution, for he was the priest from the dark church.)

36.
Not One of Us

It's great that you came back. You're so tan now. But I like it. Wait, what did you guys sell? Ah, hardware. See, you just can't escape those nuts and bolts! Went belly-up, eh? Too true. But not us! Just look at us… Heck yeah, the nineties, they ran right over us and kept on going. I got a little tired. I hightailed it out of production and went after the easy money. Never mind. You'll be irreplaceable here. We've only got a thousand people, so nobody's replaceable, anyway. And you will be our… Ah! You'll be our PR guy. We don't have any PR. We'll give you the office the Embassy of Senegal used to rent. It's a little dusty, true, and their leader's, like, magic mirror is still on the wall. All you have to do is wipe off the dust. I'll write down the instructions how to use the mirror. Just ask for the military specialists, heh heh; your wish is their command.

The Embassy of Senegal's office is dismal. The magic mirror on the wall isn't reflecting anything. The sad factory courtyard outside the window. Banded layers of dust hanging in the motionless air. Full-spectrum light bulbs raging and crackling overhead. What the heck did Danilka put in here? This *is* a factory, right? But nobody'd even dreamed of a factory back then. He opens the cabinet. Piles of old technical drawings fall out. He gathers them all up in his arms and heads out to the courtyard to the dumpster. He lights a match: *skritch*. Go on, tell me more.

Of course nobody came back. He was the only one stupid enough to do that. Life goes by so fast! Oh, yes, life, it goes by so fast! And it's so sad! So damn sad! A sad gray sky over the factory courtyard. But it's only been ten years! That's all—just ten years! (Poking with his foot at the old drawings' ashes.) A pit for the snow. A pink line on the wall. A wave of nausea rolls over him.

All at once a bizarre sight enters his peripheral vision. A strapping young buck with bad teeth is pushing a cart with a high, swaying stack of boxes covered in purple stamps. Old lady Tasya, the finisher, flutters around the cart in her great-granddaughter's raggedy old Uggs. Her makeup's a mix of harlequin and corpse. Her brows are blacked in. Hey, Z! Tasya shouts. Tell your friend to spread some gravel over here or something! Or just go ahead and lay down some asphalt! Where were you, Khodzha, in the army? Defending the motherland? The absurdity of Tasya's suggestion makes the young snaggletooth bust out into a surprisingly funny laugh. His ears, Z notices, have coins in the lobes. Want some help with that? Don't need it! The two of us, we know every little dip in the road! Let's go, C, move it! Let's go! They clang and wheeze their way over to a burrow in the side of the main building, then disappear into it. Both of them have torn-up old boots. Soon mine will be the same.

Everything on the Central Tower's staircase is the same as always. The movie posters that Director V papered all over the walls haven't faded. In the operations director's office the director of operations himself, the indomitable F, is yelling. Because this is the fourth day they haven't produced the quantity they need! No, I'm not blaming you, you've got nothing to do with it! You put in the order, and they should fill it for you. But all you guys, why the hell are you screwing around? Everybody's been working their tails off for a month! They're trying to make their deadlines! But then everything goes to shit, because of you... I don't give a crap about THAT! I already knew about that a year ago!! We transferred I and U to you, we did EVERYTHING for you! Now go and start doing your job!! Get out of here! You should be ashamed of yourselves!! With burning ears and bugged-out eyes, Shop Nine's foreman, Pal Palych P (Junior, the one who'd washed Director N's Volga), comes tumbling out of the office straight into Z. Then A, the chief dispatcher, comes flying out, with G, the foreman of Sixteen, stumbling after her, weak in the knees. Z knocks and enters. F is drinking from the spout of the teakettle. There you are, Z, you did turn up! The prodigal son! That's what I'm talking about! I told you, stick with a smokestack, sonny! Stick with a smokestack, the factory'll never let you down! Don't take it to heart, you wouldn've made director anyway! Heh, heh. Come on over tomorrow and have a good time, the kids are getting a little something together. Now scram, I've got things to do. Tell me, though, where's Simochka M these days? Did she leave? No, she's at her desk... they were moved to the internal courtyard, you know. All righty then! See you later! F abruptly stubs out his cigarette and grabs the phone: hello! (Impressionable F imitates Director N, who he started out under, with his democratic tyranny; his ability to see the person in the worker and vice versa; his mannerisms; his cigarettes; his way of addressing everyone informally, using *ty* and first names; and his hard liquor in the teakettle.)

Well then, time to see M. Best get it over with. The very first day. See her, then—to heck with her, forget her. Z enters the internal courtyard. The gates are tightly bandaged with a fire hose and have been painted shut with whitewash. A cross drawn in chalk. Z slips and falls, flailing, on the ice. His palms scalded, he leaps up like someone roughly woken from a sound sleep. The old guy remembered wrong, or something… what "internal courtyard"? Must've meant from the outside. It's three thirty, gotta hurry or she'll be gone. Z gallops back to the Central Tower and runs up to the deserted second floor (once there'd been shops and more shops here, it'd been wall-to-wall people). Seems like the through hallway used to be right around here… Is this it? No, it's this one! They repainted here, can't recognize a thing. Z heads down the hallway. Here's a turn, and another. New doors, new signs. The entrance to the green staircase. Now an odd little zig-zag: need to go up to the third floor, down the hall, and then back down to the internal courtyard. It's dark up there. That's the way it should be. It's lit up ahead. Z fumbles down the hall on the third floor by feel. Where's the dang light? Down a little staircase… the technical documentation department was here once, where the top-secret Margarita Konstantinovna used to eat documents before reading them… but now, apparently, not only does nobody work here, nobody ever comes around here at all. Z starts to feel uneasy. Nope, seems there's no entrance to the internal courtyard from here. Maybe it's at the bottom of the green staircase? Back again the same way, by feel; that's the entrance to the green staircase, already, so now it's down to the second floor… but the door, a heavy door covered with oilcloth, turns out to be locked. Somebody'd pushed the door shut while Z was wandering around the side alleys and dead ends of the technical documentation department. Or maybe it was the wind. But now there's no way to get out of here. There's no getting out of here at all.

Z sits down in a bottomed-out old armchair on the landing between the second and third floors of the green staircase. A light bulb shines wanly through the wire mesh of the broken elevator. Z lights up. It's three forty-five. She's left already, of course. It might very well be that… that nobody even comes here on a regular basis. And that means that—well, that nobody's going to show up until after New Year's. Not even Buratino's key can open this locked door for me. And Z's cell phone is back in the office. But he's not afraid.

I barely got any sleep last night. I was tossing and turning, couldn't stop thinking about something… well, sure I was thinking about M. Not about this shitty Freedom Factory, that's for sure. Basically the only reason I came here is because you gotta go somewhere. But I'm not one of them. Even back then, I wasn't one of them. I need to go off and live in a warm country, I'm half-Uzbek, half-Jew. "You're so tan now."

Dusty green light, like in the auditorium during a show's dress rehearsal. Z's thoughts ascend and intermingle majestically. He dozes off.

Z wakes up because someone is looking at him. He flinches as he opens his eyes. Two women, each with a cigarette in her fingers, stand on the third-floor landing. They look at him. Oh my goodness gracious, it's Khodzha! Z blinks. He's blinded. Forget "to heck with her." His mouth is dry. Her eyes are even greener. Z tries to speak: M. He takes off his glasses, wipes them. He rubs his bald spot. He stands up and tugs his jacket down. Easy now, need to say it just the right way. My dear M, they haven't changed you a bit.

37.

Lugs

V, the next-to-last director of the Freedom Factory, has conceived the desire to find out what the young (only 50) new director, L, is doing with the enterprise under his command. It goes without saying that Director L gives Director V the chance to do so. Director V arrives at a workshop, takes a few laps around it, examines the CNC milling machines, runs his hands over them, and gives brilliant speeches. The current director, L, walks behind him, watching. It's important to Director L that Director V appreciate his work, that Director V appreciate that L has grown up, that L has turned into a strong leader, that L has come into his own. L's passionate desire to prove this makes it perfectly clear that L has not come into his own yet.

Now here's our very own D, please give him a warm welcome. The factory's most senior machinist. How long have you been working here at this very spot? Fifty-seven years now. In this same shop. In this same spot. Actually, he and I started out together. But he went and made a career for himself, while I didn't. I just stayed here at this very same spot. Well sure, because he's a good-for-nothing, see... A good-for-nothing. Exactly. But I never... I have to make decisions all the time, decisions that… but you take our D here, he's pure as the driven snow, because he didn't make a career for himself. But what you have to remember is that when I'm not around anymore, nobody'll give a damn, but if D goes and buys the farm, the entire factory'll grind to a halt in a day. Ah, he's exaggerating. And what makes anybody think we're gonna buy the farm anytime soon? Right! We're not buying any farms! We're men at the very peak of our strength! How old were you when you came here? Fifteen, same as you. But the reason D and I came here is that we were C students and nothing in school really captured our interest. P.E., maybe… We were assigned to Danil Danilych, and he taught us all the ins and outs and little tricks of the trade. And then it was D, believe it or not, who turned out to be a model student, but I was still a bad one. So I stayed a fitter while D moved on to being a machinist. Yup, and that's the reason you made it way up there to where you are today, whereas I stayed a machinist from that day to this. My work's interesting, no other kind I'd rather do. Mine too…

And by the way, do you know how much I made back then, as a nineteen-year-old? Seventeen hundred rubles. Nice to be working back then! And it was asses to elbows, to put it plainly. Down below, the guys were standing in line at the machines. And us assemblers, well, we didn't even leave the factory at all, not on weekends and not on holidays! We never asked questions about how to do this or how to make that, either. We read the technical drawing, and if we could read it, we worked from it. We always knew what the device was. What it was for. All the technical specs. If they shot off a rocket somewhere, we'd have a little celebration. Because it was all our equipment. I remember like it was yesterday when they brought Powers down… We were the ones who riveted the cabinets for the Volkhov that did it… and we did the innards for some of them, too. Or take the Cuban missile crisis… All that geopolitics is right here, it was made by these two hands! And I had a hand in making basically 80% of all our devices! There was this pan, and you'd run over and dip every single filter in it, wash it with alcohol. My heart bled for every one of them! I remember we'd just started assembling the Golden Globe. We had quite a time with it. It's made out of stainless steel, but nobody warned us. It sat on these wheels, huge wheels, about yea big. They had to fit on real tight, but then they also had to come off without too much trouble. We started fitting one in, we're hammering it in, and nothing. It's not going in. So we head down to the first floor, where we've got our twenty-five-ton press. We put it in the press and what do you know, the wheel just burst! Looked like a broken bottle from a barfight!

Director V continues along the partition with increasing celerity and agility, getting ahead of himself. He advances chaotically to machinist Q's work station. The work station is plastered in cyber-superheroes of various Slavic nationalities. "Be a lone wolf!" is Q's motto. Seven years ago Q grew close to Yana, a salesgirl in a home appliances shop. Q pampered her and helped with her little daughter, he put up a swing at the dacha and fed the little girl wild strawberries right out of his hand. But one time Q, that fool, got into Yana's email, where he discovered she'd been exchanging sexy letters with someone, full-on slutty stuff. Then it was all over with the wild strawberries. Now the only thing at Q's dacha is some rusted bicycle chains lying around.

Former Director V, who was seldom to be seen in the workshops during his blessed reign, is advancing toward Q's station. A machinist? Marvelous! So why did you come to work in the factory? Oh, you like it, do you? Wonderful. Now you do understand, don't you, what it means to sharpen your cutter? How important it is to sharpen your cutter? Of course! That's what I use in my job every day. I think that there should be a reason for every person to live for a reason... there should be something that gives your life a reason to live... A person should have a life to live for. Yes, absolutely! affirms Director V excitedly. Bonding with those around him is part of his nature, so of course he's convinced that he's found a kindred spirit in Q. Sharpen that cutter! Director V had also been a machinist, albeit not for very long, but you can't get by without it, if you haven't been a machinist, and a little bit of an actor at the same time, you'll never become... Er, that is... So tell me, you're a young man, why didn't you go work in an office? The pay's better there, right? Oh, the nuts and bolts are more interesting? Now that's the spirit! So what do you think, what lies ahead for all of us? You know better than me, I'm an old man now, I'm eighty-five, you know, but you, what do you foresee for us? Well, well, well, that's a bit much, isn't it! What do you mean the end of the world, heh heh, don't you go spoiling my mood, brother. That's stuff and nonsense. Just look at us... you know, back in the day... rockets were going up. There was a lot of apprehension. And then, strange as it may seem, it worked out, the world got through it. And it'll get through this, too! You think we're going to move? That would be totally cool, but it's hard for me to imagine.

And so they talk on. Meanwhile, the director, Danila L, wanders around behind the neighboring machines, and underneath Q and V's conversation, his thoughts turn in a different direction: any day now a committee is coming to the factory to check on the Golden Globe and decide whether Freedom can be entrusted with producing a new, updated model. We already won the tender, but the factory's in such a state, they could easily... but maybe instead of having to drag the committee around all the workshops, it'd be better to just make a movie? Make a movie about the factory, and about the

Golden Globe, and show that to the committee? Director V did that too, back then. The committee watched the movie and was satisfied. We'll do the same thing. Because otherwise... we don't even have storage sheds for the finished Globes... and anyway... rags and alcohol everywhere, metal shavings, indecent pictures on the walls. The machinist Q is genuinely laughing for the first time in several months, and V is also laughing. Sharpen that cutter! Director V has latched on to the front of machinist Q's shirt: yes, indeed! That's just it! You're exactly right!

Through the window a light dusting of snow is visible, and the profile of a woman, composed of cracks in the asphalt across from the Central Tower, turns white, transparent, and icy.

38.

The Fuel System Maintenance and Repair Workshop of the Factory Workers!

My mama cleans the fuelsystemshop at the Freedom Factory. It's a great big field of rubber under a roof. The rubber is hard, almost like asphalt. If you get a running start and take a big jump, you can feel how it's springy under your feet. If you lie down under one of the work stations, right up under the machine where the rubber isn't worn down and dirty, you can smell the floor, and lick it. The ground there smells and tastes like rubber. In the fuelsystemshop people walk with longer and higher strides than on regular ground. It's made this way special so that the people at the factory can get from place to place faster, 'cause see the fuelsystemshop is big. I always feel like galloping and running on this rubber ground. But mama explained that's dangerous. This one lady was galloping around the fuelsystemshop and she hit her temple on a hunk of machinery and she died.

The way to get to the fuelsystemshop goes through a whole bunch of pleasant and unpleasant places. You have to breathe through your mouth at first. Other parts of the factory smell good, like bricks, or metal, or asphalt, or smoke. But there's one place, next to the big clock room where mama punches in and out, that smells really bad. So whenever we go through the clock room, I squinch up the inside of my nose beforehand and start breathing through my mouth. But my brain still remembers that smell, and so squinching up the inside of my nose beforehand doesn't really help. Then we come out into the courtyard, and I have to squinch up my eyes, because we walk past a big square pit, and one time I saw a dead cat with its guts hanging out in there. There are trees growing in the courtyard. Last fall little radioactive pears grew on them. You are not allowed to eat them, but you can have one tiny little bite. Those hard pears have an average taste. There's also hawthorn and dog rose under the pear trees, and one place where there's a barberry bush. They're all radioactive. But you can have one tiny little berry.

After the courtyard we end up in a big eight-story brick building with a tower on the roof. We push the elevator call button. The elevators in the factory are really good and I'm not afraid of them. Even though they're old, they're sturdy, they're not all loose, and they don't shake when you're riding them. There's not dirty words and pictures written and drawn all over them. There's nothing that says "Who's the biggest whore in this whorehouse?" or "Vika's a fat cow." There's no half-eaten cookies, sunflower seed shells, or cigarette butts lying around. But there is one drawback to the factory elevator: it might stop earlier than it needs to and open the door. You just have to press the button again, and then it does it right.

When you come out of the elevator onto the fifth floor, you wind up in the most marvelous place on earth. I'd like to live in this place after I die. The walls here are lined with beautiful bubbles that have a soft rosy-pink and baby-blue sheen. Each of those bubbles looks like a whole cosmos.

Then I have to cover my ears, because the way we take to get to the fuelsystemshop goes through Shop Thirty-Five, and something's always making this ominous booming sound in that shop.

And only after that shop do we finally get to the fuelsystemshop. Mama starts cleaning, but I just walk around looking at stuff and trying to find all kinds of little things: nuts, gears, wheels, pins, and other bits and pieces. Actually, I haven't been finding anything lately. Werther probably got all the bits and pieces.

I really like that last name, Werther. As a matter of fact, there are a lot of good names linked to this factory. For example: Werther, Dopkis, Zadorozhny, Fratkin, Ratmanov. These names come up in conversation when mama and other people at the factory are talking. I'd like to have such a nice last name. Instead of that I have this last name: Solomakha, from the word *soloma*. Straw. Actually, there are a lot of ugly last names at the factory. For example, Sepity. I know a man with that last name. He walks slowly in stiff pants that don't bend. Usually he doesn't say anything. I don't say hello to him. One time he said to me, just hanging around, boy? You should go help your mother. She works her fingers to the bone for you, all by herself. I was ashamed. I went over to mama and said, let me help you. But of course mama said, you're helping me by staying out of the way.

I'm not allowed to leave the fuelsystemshop while mama's working. Freedom's been a secret factory ever since Soviet times, and if I get lost inside it, nobody will look for me or ever find me. I look out the window a lot, thinking up stories about how I'd live at the factory if I ever did get lost. I think I wouldn't die. Because see, I do know where the cafeteria is, I've been there a few times, and I get to eat for free there. At night, to sleep, I'd go up to the fourth floor of the building where mama clocks in and out. The payroll department is there, and it has a long runner of soft red and green carpet leading to it. I'd roll myself up in it like the Wolf from the cartoon Just You Wait! and I'd be really comfortable, all rolled up in there. It smells very refined in the payroll department, it's an official kind of smell, linked to words like "Reichskanzler" and "secretary of the department of rusty vee and media."

One time, mama was cleaning there instead of Auntie Lyusya, and she locked me in a little office in there and gave me a pencil to draw with. I started opening all the desk drawers. One of them had matches in it. I just by accident stuck my pencil in a hole in a big metal box that I found in the wall without meaning to, and the box opened. For a long time I lit matches one by one and threw them into the metal box. I wadded up several pieces of paper that were inside the box and made a small campfire. I did everything carefully, and mama didn't see anything.

And so I'd sleep in the building with the carpet. The whole rest of the time I'd go around the factory and learn to work a machine and eventually I'd become a lathe operator. Sometimes I'd visit my mama, when she comes in to wash the floor in the fuelsystemshop.

But these are all just daydreams, and in real life I'm just afraid to go outside the fuelsystemshop by myself. Because see, to get lost I'd have to go through Shop Thirty-Five first, where there's always that ominous booming. So that's why I don't get lost, why I always stay in the very same place, the fuelsystemshop, and why I sometimes get bored there.

There's a dusty old neglected hunk of machinery in the most neglected corner of the fuelsystemshop. There used to be a whole bunch of little metal bits and pieces scattered around it, but I collected them all, so now it's as boring there as it is everywhere else. But one good thing is that the floor there is still more rubbery than in the rest of the fuelsystemshop, and more yellow. So you can jump really high on the floor right by the neglected hunk of machinery. And also, behind the big piece of metal, there's a little stack of neglected signboards made of fabric stretched over thin panels of wood. They're really dusty, but if you sit down and try, you can read them, there's writing on them in white letters. This is what's written on them:

"Don't allow an increase in idle time!"
"No production defects for a strong home front!"
"Follow our procedures! The enemy"

And there's also a smaller wooden panel there, that has the words "of the factory workers!" on it.

But once I got so bored it was just a nightmare, so I found mama and began begging and pleading, please, mama, please can I go for a walk, just as far as the elevators? I want to spend a little while there on the stairs where the walls are covered in bubbles. I won't get lost, I'm begging you, I walk that same path all the time! You know I do! All right, mama said. Just as long as you don't go anywhere else. Just go there for a little while and then come right back.

I walked up to the door that leads to Shop Thirty-Five. My heart started pounding really hard. I covered my ears good and tight, threw my whole body against the door, and took off running as soon as the door opened. The floor in Thirty-Five isn't rubber, it's concrete and full of cracks, and so I ran really fast, making big leaps as I ran so I wouldn't step on any cracks, and I kept my ears covered the whole time. I raced lightning fast through Thirty-Five and jumped out into the stairwell where the elevators are, and there I was in that miraculous place I love so much.

It was quiet and cold there, and it smelled like it usually does at the factory: like brick, concrete, and scorched cable, and also like fresh wind and fresh snow from outside. I stood in that magical place for a very long time, admiring the bubbles on the walls and the high ceiling with cobwebs growing on it, and listening to the booming in Shop Thirty-Five, sounding like it was coming from the great beyond, but it wasn't scary to hear from all the way over here.

Then the elevator doors slid apart and two nice little fat ladies in white lab coats came out, jostling each other cheerfully. Well of course, one of them said. The other one said, and then the folks who live in the big city, like Moscow, you say they're from Moscow Shitty. The first one laughed and said, but no, really, I mean it, maybe if we sink all the money into that, they won't…

But I didn't hear any more, because they both slipped off into Shop Thirty-Five. They were so calm going into that terrible place that I realized it's good to be cheerful. So I resolved to be cheerful from then on, to collect jokes and funny stories. And I also resolved right there and then that on my way back I wouldn't run through Shop Thirty-Five with my ears covered up like a coward, I would walk through it, calm and collected, as though I worked there.

But just then the elevator doors slid apart again, and a man who looked kind of like a monkey stepped out onto the fifth floor. Whose are you, he said. I replied: this is a secret factory, and that's secret, too. The man laughed. Then he looked at his watch and said, have you seen the compass? I said, I don't know. The man said, knucklehead! Put it this way: have you been up on the tower? Tell me quick, I've got to be somewhere in twenty minutes… I haven't, I said quickly. Then let's go have a look. We went up. On the eighth floor we got out of the elevator, walked down a very clean, low corridor, and then climbed up a metal ladder. The man opened a hatch and clambered out onto the roof. I clambered out after him.

We were on the roof, right up under the sky, out in the

snow. Neither of us had a jacket. But I knew for sure that we wouldn't catch cold, because people don't catch cold at a time like this! We were on the roof! The guy swept his hand over the whole entire district and said, well here we are, on the tower! And that is the Compass!

I saw the Compass. It consisted of an enormous roundish-square antenna. Quietly, without a sound, the Compass rotated on top of a long, tall rod. What's it for? I asked. If it's bad weather and just one little hostile ship gets it into its head to cross the Gulf separating us from them, the Compass will let us know immediately. But what if it's a friendly little ship in good weather? All the more so. We'll put on the teakettle and set out some cookies.

My feet were sinking into the snow. The gray sky above us looked pinkish. The tower with the Compass was very high up. I saw the Narva Gates, and the square, and the cathedral, and even the train station. We didn't spend very much time on the roof at all. That's it, let's go, said the man. He herded me back through the hatch and took me back down to the fifth floor. As we parted, I said, well, might as well introduce ourselves! My name is Sasha Solomakha. Who are you? I'm Fratkin, said the man. I said, nice to meet you, I've heard of you. I'd really like to be Fratkin. Or Werther. Fratkin said, well, now! I'd also like to be Werther, but I'm just Fratkin. It could be worse. Why don't we let everybody be who they are: I'll be Fratkin, and you be Solomakha. I said, I don't like my name. It comes from the word for straw. No, it doesn't come from the word *soloma*, it comes from the word *solo*, meaning one, and *makhach*, meaning a fight. So that means that you can win against many, even if you're fighting by yourself. Got it? Got it, I said.

39.

Intermedio.

regardless like let's speak frankly I took those steps through the exact same sort of like yeah jobs, the rungs of the ladder, and that's why I like I don't know I collected kind of like statistics, something like that yeah you know like that structural system that administrative system how it all works you know for what it's worth well it's probably worth knowing all that but well no need to know all that // forgive me, please, forgive me for not rushing out to see you my last appointment of the day's to revel in the sea view it can't be sipped like light, this clear and bright autumnal wine, but black as night, as burning bright, flows this autumnal wine the distant paths stretch on and cross the border of the day postponement of the night is good and takes the pain away // in fact the factory is a kind of like you know a model for me a model of like our nation strange as it may seem a model of that like you know I don't remember exactly lars von trier one of his first films was about a psychiatric hospital it was called the kingdom it was a television series I don't remember he described that model of a society that actually exists in reality a model of our nation in particular because this factory is in our nation and all those same vices are inherent to us and we have a socium here

too we have bureaucracy that well like as a matter of fact everything is saturated with it and we see corruption because
wherever there's bureaucracy there's corruption we see love
here too probably that's like enough the nation is these four
like kind of like walls that you can take and turn this way
and that on the table and imagine that it's the society that
we kind of like live in strange as it may seem I also see it
well at least that's what it seems like to me // I'm not one of
them, I'm different, my heart pumps another, altered blood
the way the factory's boiler room pumps rusty, scalding fluid
these people all these nuts and bolts they're nobody's they're
not my people but this is my career and my keys are on a
string around my neck as though I wasn't hopeless as though
I could unlock my happiness // yeah we make instruments
we make products we even deliver them to our customers
who then put them to use but is there really any point to
it I think not because these products they aren't planes that
bring passengers out of some place that's like hard to get to
and it's not like we're you know like such altruists our products are pretty much all weapons designed to do what exactly well as they say you know yourself what they're designed
to do and therefore considering that we aren't currently living in a time of war when like you know every single like
hour we waste would be equivalent to sort of like betrayal
or desertion we make what nobody well right what nobody
needs these days it's like well you know it's like you know
I call it a museum it's kind of like a naval museum that like
yeah you can build it up as much as you want but these days
it's not bringing in either profit or expenses nope nothing so
well right so you see that's why there's like nothing really to
be said about it // I dreamed of creamy white of unyielding
lines taut-strung strings far beyond the horizon and there's a
dripping a dripping beneath my feet and inside ripe plums

the pits are peeping and I'm walking along empty and stern like cellophane sandpaper I polish steel with a touch and a thick slab of sunlight's slathered on it I don't have to handle the branches it's okay they won't grow through me and see these towers and these waterways I won't outgrow them // put it this way the people who like ended up here at the factory with us well once they saw all this it's not like it like grabbed them but they just you know kind of get stuck here for a while but this while it's like sometimes like every once in a while this while's enough to well see once you've forgotten to answer the question why am I here it's enough to just stay here although saying that isn't exactly like the best way to go about it of course it's not like the best course to hold in life that's just like the duds the ones we've got here at the factory people with any kind of ambition at all would never work here cause like because you do run into perfectly fine people who do have like some ambition and they're like can I live on this much money no I can't and that's why well thank god the folks in human resources don't ask themselves these kinds of questions they don't feel the pangs of conscience in this regard if you don't like it leave although to tell the truth it's like well if I was walking out of an HR department like that I would leave I'd just like keep on walking // oh, if only I could leave walk away then I'd have left and walked away ages ago I wouldn't have woken anybody up I'd have just left and walked away but I'm going to leave and walk away anyway // what I'd do is I'd build Disneyland here at least then it'd be useful and this place the factory would bring in some money at least although I already scoped out another place that's a little better one of the enterprises in our group has the exact same kind of factory but it does one better than us it still has its Young Pioneers campground they today they're trying to find a way to use it if you send a top-level executive out there it'd definitely end up a Disneyland for sure well like if this was a different country a different people / / I want some balloons and balls of smoke I want some cartoons and popsicles and everything I'm not allowed to have but there's nothing I'm not allowed to have it's nothing I can't live this way I can't live another day said a guy and picked up an ax I can't live this way I can't live another day said another guy and he is still alive today although it's hardly life living this way the Enola Gay even blew Hiroshima away but you leave it alone / / why I work so hard here yeah I work hard but what else can I do I mean like I work and I never leave the factory like on time right and in my own mind that means well it means that I simply can't do the work that I'm doing like I mean I can't do a bad job because like you always have a choice you spend the whole day from eight in the morning to like nine ten at night and I mean I think there's just a kind of like moral satisfaction in the fact that I spend days on end at the factory and you know I'll tell you there's a way in which I've told you right that for me the factory is a continuation of my father and a lot more we made a movie in the factory we created exhibits for a trade show and we held a trade show and we did a lot more all for our sort of like corporation it was kind of like teambuilding there are a lot of talented people and stuff and here at the factory we have well not to put too fine a point on it we have me and the other people who can do that we are doing that for us it's not well I mean it's not like a huge effort and the people who get who've gotten sort of like deep down inside themselves l mean like self-actualized kind of and I realized that it's kind of like oh and also there's this kind of like way let's say where we sort of get these like certain emotions let's say that you're somehow like supposed to get in like this one particular place well I mean usually you know what I mean so like yeah but the factory is doomed its future's already decided no point in talking about it

---

he walks around with this little notebook that looks like a well-worn library copy of Chernyshevsky's *What Is to Be Done*: hard-cover, cover art, bookmark, everything was imitated with the utmost precision, so when you ask him what he's doing with his *What Is to Be Done*, is he reading it or something? he answers, "Nope, writing," and he opens up the day planner for you, kilometers of empty pages, which will still, sooner or later, come to an end

40.

Engineer H

His whole life, Aitch had always had that feeling of something lacking, a scarcity of life energy, as though the stream flowing through him was dull and narrow. Maybe this was because Aitch's childhood had passed in those hard years when they only ate apples, potatoes, bread, and cabbage, and primarily drank (apart from alcohol) water mixed with five-minute blackberry jam. Aitch had been short and thin his whole life. He wore his pale hair short, and had begun balding not long after twenty-five. He'd expected no better of himself. Aitch had been dealt a tough hand, with neither father nor siblings, neither an attractive appearance nor special talents. But he hadn't been dealt an utterly hopeless hand, either: neither despair, nor poverty, nor stupidity. No, Aitch was secretly rather smart about some things, and occasionally very sensitive, and he wasn't without a sense of humor, lackluster though it be (for his own personal consumption, since Aitch was fairly reticent).

Still, it wasn't as though this something lacking made Aitch depressed. He didn't even think about stuff like that. Aitch ate what was served; did what he was supposed to; wrote out the solutions to math problems with a cheap blue ballpoint pen, the end of which he was always chewing on;

lugged around a worn-out blue rucksack on his skinny back; got up early and ate breakfast in the kitchen, brimming with blue shadows; and ran, cringing from the cold, down the old, dark stairs. Aitch didn't stand out in school, either in the regular neighborhood one, or in the special math school he transferred to in eighth grade. Still, he wasn't totally devoid of distinguishing characteristics. Overall, he was a great kid, sensible and level-headed, not like the quietest guy you'd ever met, but a regular guy: he sticks his hand out to shake yours, to say hi, and he's always up for a little soccer, and he's totally able to keep up his side of the conversation. He was even in the top ten students in the class, up there in the top third with Petrov, Ivanov, and so forth (whenever the teacher listed the names, Aitch wasn't mentioned, but was always implied).

And that feeling of something lacking? Well, every so often Aitch would think, "what am I so skinny for?" And sometimes he'd feel something similar, he'd feel like there was something else that he could have more of; that he had the capacity for this inside him, these little green underdeveloped shoots, like if somebody who was color-blind suddenly dreamed in red and green, and then woke up, confused: What was that? What's it called? But his feeling wasn't quite that strong; it was light, almost weightless; but continual, like a hum, like dust.

Later Aitch went to university, in engineering, of course, and he was an okay student, took his notes in his chicken-scratch handwriting; he never got a sense of what he wanted to be, he didn't think about it, he just had his little jobs here and there, helped his mom, but then one time in his final year he heads in to the department to discuss the topic of his seminar paper and his advisor goes, want to write your thesis at the Freedom Factory? They're working up some new piece of equipment, you can get a respectable thesis out of it after-

wards, and at the same time you'll learn the ropes and maybe even get tapped to come on board, they need engineers. Of course, thank you very much, said Aitch, heartily grateful, and headed for Freedom.

Aitch was struck by the sight of Freedom: the enormous empty workshops, the shadows of former grandeur. The one who showed him around the factory was, of course, none other than D the Odessan, gesturing eloquently and invoking modernization, innovative industrial policies, and support for the army, Ford, and Peter the Great. Aitch hemmed and hawed, dug his stiff, open palms into his jacket pockets, and displayed a general lack of enthusiasm. This majestic, run-down Freedom was clearly not a good fit for the scrawny young engineer. And besides, this Freedom's such a desert. Eight thousand workers this factory used to have, but now? A thousand. The Experimental Design Bureau used to have eight hundred people in it, but now there's forty. The future is unclear. Still, D said excitably, we have a new project now. Yes, that's right. The first one in many years. In our very own EDB. We're just starting work. Want to start with us? It's called the Compass. It's a radar system, it'll be in all kinds of ports, on embankments and lighthouses. It's highly promising. Of course, thank you, said Aitch. And smiled, kind of. Or not. Doesn't matter.

The upshot is that he fit in to that bureau like a hand in a glove, and started working on that same Compass. He was a unit finisher. That means that, say, something doesn't work, but the way it doesn't work is different every time. And Aitch was the one who had to figure out why. He had to put a shine on shit, as the saying goes… but he didn't just fit in, he really got into it. Suddenly, it turned out that all that inconceivable knowledge the university had crammed into him was really in him, in his hands and eyes. The Compass grew.

Two years later they finished developing it and handed it over to production. Now Aitch was stuck in the shops for days at a time, rather, in Shop Nineteen, where they were doing the final assembly of the very first Compass. Every morning at seven thirty he turned onto Volynkina from Strike Prospect, stormed up the incline, and was at Freedom by fifteen to eight. The pay wasn't that much. Aitch knew he could make more. But he was drawn to the work. Not that much, just a little, just enough to keep him there.

And then there was the soccer. Whenever the guys got a game together, Aitch was there. He'd always loved to kick the ball around. Aitch's normally hidden, effaced qualities emerged when he played soccer: his cunning, his keen sense of his surroundings and love of paradox, his buoyance and transparence. When he played, his eyes went from gray to steely (although it may seem to some that gray and steely are the same). It may be that he was lacking in force, expression, drive, ambition; but Aitch's movements were always spare and finely honed, he unfailingly intuited the intentions of both friends and enemies, and his play was like speed chess. Freedom would've beat the Putilov factory hands down with Aitch, of course, but unfortunately Freedom was forced to win without him. During one of the last scrimmages somebody let Aitch fall, or maybe he fell by himself—basically the guys got too into the game, and it ended up with Aitch laying on the sand and pine needles, holding his foot, his face horribly contorted.

It took him a month to heal, the rest of September and all of October, so that when Aitch was finally given his freedom and he made it past the intersection and stormed up Volynkina—without a trace of a limp, by the way—he noticed that the trees in Ekaterinhof Park had already lost all their leaves and that only in the hedges did the occasional wet red or yellow leaf still glisten. Aitch walked, not noticing how much he was enjoying the neighborhood, and the autumn, and the beloved, familiar scenery he was observing for the third autumn, while off in the distance Freedom's tall towers soared, and there, on that tower, his Compass was waiting for him, the one that'd been installed up there, and on the embankment, too, while he was out sick. Aitch skirted the entry hall and went up to the third floor. Everybody in the EDB was happy to see him, and he was happy to see them. He wiped the dust off his computer screen and turned it on. They were beginning development on a new project, a continuation of the Compass that promised many more years of interesting work. The tower, have you been up on the tower yet? asked Lida M. Oh! You haven't been yet! Go on, then. Go on up to the tower, if your foot's okay, of course. Thanks, yeah, my foot's okay; that's right, I will go have a look at what we've all been cobbling together these past few years.

The tower where they'd installed the very first Compass unit was an ancient tower. It was left from back when Freedom had housed a textile factory. It had been spared in 1942 by the shelling that had obliterated half of Freedom's workshops, since the artillery aimed by it. Aitch climbed out onto the roof and saw the radar station in all its glory. He looked at it for a while, then turned around and stood gazing out at the city. He felt good.

Out of nowhere that feeling of something lacking, that feeling that'd been the main thing about him his whole life, seemed to light up the whole world, as if he'd subtly turned a key; everything still fell a little short, but that was wonderful. It's good to live, for as long as you need to, and you won't change, almost at all, the way you didn't change up till now, and that keenness, the flow of time, the warm, crisp air moving in currents around you, those gray and white trails of smoke that contain the whole spectrum, and the Compass, and the new project ahead of you, and the short, gnarled brooms of the poplars on clean-swept Strike Prospect, and the pale lilac sky above the city... all that actually *is* [...]

Saint Petersburg, 2012

Biographies

Poet, fiction writer, and artist **Ksenia Buksha** was born in Saint Petersburg. She holds a degree in economics from Saint Petersburg State University and has worked as a journalist, copywriter, and day trader. Since her breakout fiction collection *Alyonka the Partisan* (2002), Buksha has been winning acclaim as a brilliant stylist and satirist whose linguistic experimentation is guided by a healthy sense of the absurd. In 2014, *The Freedom Factory* won the National Bestseller award and was a finalist for the Big Book Award. Buksha's work has been translated into Polish, Chinese, French, and English.

Anne O. Fisher's recent translations include works by Sigizmund Krzhizhanovsky, Nilufar Sharipova, Ilya Danishevsky, Aleksey Lukyanov, and Julia Lukshina. Fisher and co-translator Derek Mong collaborated to produce *The Joyous Science: Selected Poems of Maxim Amelin* (White Pine Press, 2018), awarded the 2018 Cliff Becker Prize. Fisher is Senior Lecturer in the Department of Translation and Interpreting Studies at the University of Wisconsin-Milwaukee.

CPSIA information can be obtained
at www.ICGtesting.com
Printed in the USA
LVHW050459201218
601121LV00006B/9/P